INSIGNIFICANT GESTURES

INSIGNIFICANT GESTURES

JO CANNON

Published by
Pewter Rose Press
17 Mellors Rd,
West Bridgford
Nottingham, NG2 6EY
United Kingdom
www.pewter-rose-press.com

First published in Great Britain 2010

ISBN 978-0-9560053-5-9

British Library Cataloguing in Publication Data
A catalogue record for this book is available from the British Library

Cover design by www.thedesigndepot.co.uk
Printed and bound in Great Britain

Pewter Rose Press
www.pewter-rose-press.com

CONTENTS

Insignificant Gestures   1

New Look   9

Rictus   14

Evo-Stik and the Bigamist   22

Theresa's Spear   31

Nasma's Malady   38

Eye of the Storm   44

The Alphabet Diet   53

Daddy's Girl   61

Needle-Stick Baby   68

Running On The Right Side Of The Brain   74

The Crow Down The Chimney   79

One Hundred Days   87

Pump It Up   94

Stalker   100

Hand Of God   102

A Good Match   110

Shutters   117

Love On The Rocks   125

Mercy is Sick Today   129

The Spaces Between   131

Fairy Story   138

Salt Man   144

Staying Power   150

Jam   157

ACKNOWLEDGEMENTS

Stories in this collection were previously published in: *The Reader, Brand magazine, Myslexia, Cadenza, The New Writer, Willesden Herald Anthology 2010, Route 'Book at Bedtime,' Fish Anthology 2007, Leaf Anthology 2007, Momaya Annual Review 2006, Earlyworks 'Survival Guides', Decongested tales, Cinnamon Press anthology.*

They appeared on-line in *Pank* and *Right Hand Pointing.*

Stories were placed or short-listed in the following competitions: *Fish International, Brit Writers Award, HISSAC, City of Derby, Frome Festival, Lichfield and District Festival, Ilkley Festival, Biscuit, Cafe Writers, Writers Bureau.*

I would like to thank the following people for their help in my writing life:

Anne and Nick McDonnell of Pewter Rose Press for this wonderful opportunity.

Dear friend and poet Carolyn Fisher (*the Unsuspecting Sky*) for her interest in every word.

John Haigh, for that pep-talk.

Gillie Bolton (*Reflective Practice: Writing and Professional Development*)

Moira Brimicombe and friends in the Sheffield reflective writing group.

Vanessa Gebbie, Val Waterhouse, Cassandra Passerelli and all my comrades on 'Fiction Forge' for generous support and help.

Zoe King for perceptive advice.

Hilary Johnson's Author's Agency
Jenni Levine for her steadfast belief in my writing.
My dear sons, Jacob and Rowan, for their enthusiasm.
Peter, the love of my life, for everything.

INSIGNIFICANT GESTURES

When I returned from Malawi I retrained as a
psychiatrist. I never wanted to smell blood again, or the
sweet nail varnish odour of starvation. Or any other stench
of human suffering. I couldn't bear to witness another
death. Of course it's different here. Some people die
quietly, with family beside them and a syringe driver
supplying regular shots of heroin. Do they float in dreams,
or does the involuting mind fasten on one last image?

If so, mine would be Celia. Her face has been with me
every day for ten years. The slightest nudge sends my
thoughts sliding down and round to their invariable end
point. From every angle, again and again, I've seen her
head arched back, bruises that bloomed beneath her skin,
her clenched hands. If I could peel back time I'd do things
differently. But you don't get second chances.

I barely recognise the man I was then. A thin strand of
consciousness is all that connects us. As if from a distance
I see myself step between patients on their straw mats,
believing I could make a difference. I remember evenings
spent drawing by oil lamp in my little whitewashed house,
while an African sunset poured itself out on the sky and
music drifted from the bars in the market. As I sketched
my intricate pictures, my mind moved like a firefly in loops
and ellipses away from the day's work. I haven't drawn
anything for ten years.

The first time I realised Celia was watching I was an
hour into a drawing. Since my teens I had covered sheet
after sheet of paper with interwoven figures — birds,

1

flowers, fantastical creatures. That evening I became aware of her warmth and quiet breathing. Beginnings start like this, with insignificant gestures: a woman's hand touching the back of a chair. Yet Celia was barely a woman. Nobody knows their age there, but she was about sixteen, eighteen at most. She was the servant who came with the house that came with my job, District Health Officer at the absurdly young age of twenty eight. Things were clearer then, I've lost my old certainty. Servants were a symbol of inequality and exploitation and I didn't need one. Until the hospital matron took me aside, as she did many times that first year, and explained.

"You've got plenty of money, Doctor. You're a single man. Celia's brothers and sisters depend on her."

So Celia stayed. She slept in a little room in the garden and walked home to her mother's thatched mud-brick hut at weekends. I grew accustomed to her amiable presence, toneless humming and faint aroma of wood smoke. I asked little of her; my life was simple and working long hours I didn't make much mess. Celia swept red dust from the concrete floors, and washed and ironed my clothes. She grew vegetables in the garden, but ashamed to let a servant prepare my solitary meals, I cooked them myself. She spent time by the gate chatting to passersby on the way to market or hospital. And later she would sit on the back step sketching with the drawing materials I gave her.

It was a small shock that first time, a few months after I arrived, to feel her watching with such concentration. I pulled a chair up beside me and indicated the pens and paper. She understood immediately and began to draw a flower, in such delicate detail I was astonished. For an hour she was completely engrossed. And so it went on, month after month, with no words exchanged between us, no judgements or calculations. I remember how every object on the table leaked a black shadow away from the lamplight; the occasional brilliance of a firefly; Celia's strange buzzing hum as she drew. I'm no longer capable of such absorption and the medication that helps me sleep makes my fingers tremble. But I'd take anything not to wake at three in the morning with my thoughts crawling round and around like caterpillars along the rim of a glass, endlessly circling the same regrets.

I knew what the staff said, but they were wrong. An African hospital is as much a gossip factory as any other. I tired of nurses rolling their eyes at me and suppressing laughter. Celia was my companion; our elbows at the table never touched. I marvelled that with only three years of schooling she could draw so well. She was a natural.

I had developed a cockroach phobia. At night I imagined them chewing through the mosquito net to hang from my lips or gnaw my foot soles. Hearing their sinister rustle in the kitchen, I'd lie awake unable to bear the tension. Then I'd spring from bed and smash them with a shoe, disgusted as much by my violence as the white sticky glue that oozed from the splattered bodies. But the next night they were back, extending feelers from beneath the toilet seat, jostling in the teapot or moving together like a glistening carpet inside the wardrobe. One evening, as Celia and I sat drawing, a gecko ran across the ceiling with a cockroach in its mouth. Pausing above my head, it devoured the insect with such gusto that legs and shredded carapace showered the paper. My chair crashed to the floor as I leapt backwards. Celia covered her face and rocked with laughter. Afterwards she seemed to feel she had to protect me from cockroaches. Every day she sought them out, stamped on dozens and swept the crushed bodies into the dust outside. The carnage appalled me, but secretly I was touched.

Sometimes the medical assistants called me at night. In the absence of phones or bleeps they sent the ambulance, a battered Land Rover, to fetch me. The vehicle would rattle round the back of the house and park with its headlights flooding my bedroom. Even now, when a passing car lights up my wall, I jerk awake with a cold rush. On the short bumpy ride to hospital I used to dread what lay ahead. At night it was never easy. There might be a protracted labour or difficult caesarean in progress and I'd scrub up and work in thick surgical gloves that were too big, with blunt instruments and scissors that didn't meet, in the overwhelming metallic reek of blood. More daunting for my colleagues was an illness, not necessarily serious, of a local politician or his relative. If anything went wrong they would be punished by exile to a hospital in the far reaches of the country. Medical assistants and nurses were moved like furniture, with no consideration for family ties. In my position of expatriate doctor working for an aid agency, I could stand between them and the politicians.

My life has drained towards one scene: the night they brought me to the ward for Celia. She was unrecognisable. Eyes swollen shut, bruised, unconscious. Her slender neck bent back like a broken sunflower. A few hours previously she'd gone home early for the weekend, carrying a bundle of cloth on her head that she'd bought for her mother in the market.

"What happened?"

4

The nurses were shocked. They'd heard the story from the village women.

"Her mother found her like this, behind their hut. They say her boyfriend beat her up. The police have caught him already."

I could feel the sick heat of her through my rubber gloves. My hands trembled but the lumbar puncture needle went in at the third attempt. A racket started in my head. We couldn't help her here. I lacked the skills to treat such a serious head injury. Perhaps in the city hospital, two hours up the road, someone could save her. That place was a stinking hell ship where she might not see nurse or medical assistant for days. But what else could I do? As usual the phones were down. There was no one to ask for advice. I sent the cerebrospinal fluid sample with the nurse who accompanied her in the Land Rover, hoping it might help.

Next morning the District Chief of Police, a fat man sweating in a dark suit, called me to his office and took down my statement in laborious long hand.

"Was there evidence of injury on the girl?"

I told him about the coma and the bruises.

After I signed the statement he took from his desk drawer two bottles of Fanta. He opened both and placed one in front of me, adding to his a tot of something from beneath the table. He pointed to mine but I shook my head.

"We've got the boy," he said.

Matron had told me about the prisons of this country, after checking over both shoulders for spies and closing my office door. There were special agents paid by politicians everywhere, even among the hospital staff.

She said, "Convicts always die, Doctor. They don't get enough to eat. Cholera or TB finishes them. The guards are cruel. No one gets out."

And I was glad. Desire for revenge had set like lava around my heart. I couldn't think straight, didn't sleep or eat. I was all edge and scalded surface. My colleagues tiptoed round me and nobody mentioned her name.

After a few days Celia's younger sister appeared in my house and began sweeping the floor.

Six weeks later I opened my mail to find a discharge summary from the city hospital.

'Celia Dimba was admitted unconscious and died two hours later. The CSF sample grew meningococcus.'

My body changed temperature as if I'd missed my footing on a flight of stairs. Now I remembered. She'd gone home early that afternoon because she felt unwell. Celia died of meningitis — I might have saved her with an injection of penicillin. I'd acted on a second hand story from frightened village women. And then I remembered the boy.

The police chief was unperturbed.

"Of course, Doctor," he murmured, when I said I wanted to change my statement and that the boy should be released.

But he didn't write anything down.

It happened a long time ago. Some days I don't think about it. When I do, heat washes through me again, right into the bones of my face and skull. Sometimes this happens on and off all day, in the minutes between patients when my mind is unconstrained. Or I wake taut and tingling as if bound in hot bandages. That's why I don't draw any more — I fear the places my thoughts go when set free. I'm a good psychiatrist and in a few years will be a consultant. Empathising with my patients' turmoil is easy. Nothing surprises me. They use bold capital letters while my writing is small and secretive, but the content is the same.

One night recently I was called to the acute ward to section a man the police had found *'wandering disturbed in a public place'*. It's a dirty business. You coax someone to reveal the secrets of his inner world, and then use the evidence to detain him. A necessary violation; the poor bastard by then is a danger to himself or others. Only the desperately ill get a section these days. Psychiatric beds are so few I spend my time trying to keep people out. After the police had gone and the disorientated patient escorted to his room to be sedated, I lingered at the nurses' station too tired to go home. The ward was hot; I wanted a crack to open and let in air. The lamp made a puddle of light on the desk, reminding me of Africa. I doodled sleepily on a scrap of paper and watched a bird take shape beneath my hand. Suddenly a cockroach crawled across the desk. I leapt up with a yelp and my chair fell back with a crash.

"You're a big man to be scared of a little beetle. You should see the size of them back home."

An African nurse stood in the doorway laughing. Her familiar accent unlocked me — I had to smile. I recognised the neatness of head and delicacy of features, the precise bark brown shade of skin. She flicked the cockroach nonchalantly onto the floor and crushed it beneath her shoe.

"Zikomo kwambiri," I hazarded.

"Don't mention it, Doctor," she replied. "And when did you learn Chichewa?"

Celia's eyes. Celia's smile.

I told her. Like opening an overhead locker, I didn't expect so much to fall out. The nurse perched on the desk, watching my face and chewing the side of her thumb. Beginnings start like this, with insignificant gestures.

NEW LOOK

The doctor is uneasy. I make people feel like that. Before they recognise and disguise it, I sense the first flicker of disquiet.

"What made you decide to have the test now?" she asks.

"I got the letter and read the leaflet. It seems sensible. Cancer prevention and all that," I say.

"But you've not had one before and you're..." She studies the computer screen. "Nearly sixty."

"I was never called in before."

She seems to have difficulty meeting my eyes. "The computer must have generated the letter when you joined the list. Do you know what the test involves?"

I nod.

She stalls, eyeing my wrists and hands. "We don't have your old records yet. Is there anything I need to know? Your medical history?"

I smile. "No. With all due respect, I tend to avoid doctors."

"Very wise."

She becomes brisk.

"OK, if you're sure. Would you like to hop up on the couch? Slip your things off. You can cover yourself with the sheet."

I obey quietly. Time decelerates. As if dream falling, the inevitable impact approaches slowly. I hear water splash as the doctor washes her hands, the clink of metal, paper rip as she opens a packet. I tell myself it's normal, an ordinary test that all women have, like a blood pressure check.

Normal.

The doctor appears between the curtains around the couch, gazing at the wall behind me. She moves the sheet that covers my thighs, hesitates, and then replaces it carefully, smoothing out the creases.

She says, "Joy, not all women need this test. Not everyone. You know that, don't you?"

I wait for a hint of derision or pity, but there's only trained, cautious neutrality.

"If you make another appointment, we can talk about this. Maybe your old notes will have arrived by then."

I won't be around that long.

My job allows me to keep moving. Every six months or so I find another furnished room or flat. In this city it's easy — you move a mile, even a few streets, and disappear. By the time people realise, draw conclusions and make judgements, I've gone. In each new place I take the mirrors down. Working from home, I write advertising copy for laboratory equipment and translate it into French. Although my scientific vocabulary is extensive, I've never been to France and would struggle to hold a conversation. I haven't met my employer, we communicate by e-mail, but the cheque paid into my account every month is ample.

The trudge of my work suits me. Days pass as hunched over my laptop, I strive for the correct word or phrase. Sometimes, surfacing, I find myself singing. Although the timbre is not to my liking, my voice is good. My mother sang. So I'm not unhappy. I know which streets and parks to avoid and never leave home after dark. A solitary life, but I'm used to it. I don't expect to have friends. My dealings with others are skewed and ambiguous, for who would be seen with me?

Late at night, after a productive day, I fetch the full length mirror from behind the wardrobe and prop it against the wall. From under the bed I take clothes still in plastic bags from New Look or Next. After lighting candles I dress carefully in underwear and slip. I like dresses that shimmer and cling — too youthful of course, but I don't wear them outside. In tights and heels I'm a little old fashioned. I observe myself in the mirror, not closely. I admire details: a perfect buckle, the gleam of a bangle in the candle light. Like any woman my age, it's best to focus on the positive. In the day I wear trousers, and apply lipstick without looking. When I'm done I undress, fold everything, replace the mirror behind the wardrobe and if I'm lucky, sleep.

When I came to this city I was young, still connected to the life pulsing through me. I took risks. In bars and clubs I'd flick open like a fan. I learned fast: a broken tooth, a damaged ear — it could have been worse. Now I'm older it's bearable. I've grown used to myself. The yearning and desperation have eased. The monotonous thoughts that crank round and around until I'd rather die than think them again, consume me less. My dreams are more orderly. But some days still I wake into a furnace. I need to be seen. If I try hard enough, walk correctly and wear the right clothes, surely someone will witness. If not, my smelting is endless.

This morning is one of those days. Too distracted to work, I find myself in New Look. The clothes are for teenagers, but older women shop there too. The tacky, glittery glamour excites me. There's a new girl at the checkout. She glances up as I reach the front of the queue. Her eyelids flicker slightly, but she smiles.

"Do you think this scarf works with my dress?" I ask.

I hear my voice pleading. An onlooker inside me contracts like a snail.

She regards me thoughtfully, then picks up the scarf and runs it though her fingers. Her face remains open. The queue stirs, but she doesn't look over my shoulder to catch someone's eye as they usually do.

"Yes, they match. It's a lovely colour," she says.

My legs are weak with gratitude and relief. I walk to the door, alert to the faintest snigger behind me, but there's none.

On a bench outside New Look I examine my purchase. I wind the scarf, a delicate spill of scarlet, through broad fingers which even with manicured painted nails resemble my father's. I consider the girl at the checkout. My mother, I imagine, might have looked like her. I don't have a photograph. She left a note for my father, not me, the day I returned from school to find him home early, waiting.

He said, "She's gone to France with her fancy man. She won't be back."

For years I wondered if he murdered her. I imagined France like heaven. Surely she'd have written if she could. I was her only child. She protected me from my father's moods and disappointment. How could she abandon me? I spent the rest of my childhood hiding from him, and grew inward and strange. Certain thoughts, like moths, began to lay the eggs that would hatch and chew my mind flimsy as lace. My mother had guessed. When she caught me at her mirror applying lipstick, I was ten. She laughed and

12

hugged me tight. But she was pretending; soon after, she went away. A red scarf and gold bangle, her clear voice singing, are all I remember now.

Searching through my handbag for the receipt I find the cervical screening leaflet and read it again. Suddenly I'm laughing nervously. Women my age are beleaguered. Bladder weakness, cancer, prolapsing parts — I'm aghast. Recalling the ominous clinking behind the doctor's curtain, the glimpse of toothed metal, I feel a faint, unprecedented affection for the shaved, redundant rod of flesh that every morning I tape flat against my thigh. With no potential to bleed or drop out, it can't harm anyone now.

I return to the checkout. The girl is still there, but the queue has gone.

"Can I bring this back? It's too young for me really," I say.

She smiles and shrugs, running my debit card though the machine.

I say, "I went for a smear test yesterday. The doctor couldn't do it."

For a moment she's perplexed, then catches my mood and laughs with me, her hand over her mouth.

"What did he say?" Her tone is gossipy, fascinated.

"*She* said, not everybody needs one."

Her laughter floats me out of the shop and back to my flat. As I open the door I start to sing, proud of my baritone.

RICTUS

The first time the dog had a fit, Dawn thought, so that's what I look like. She watched the ugly movements in dismay until at last, damp with sweat, the animal slept. Dawn wiped foam from his lips, then fetched a bucket and sponged urine from the kitchen floor.

At the chemist's, collecting her month's supply of medication, she mentioned the fit to Annie. The chemist's assistant knew something about everything but particularly, dogs.

"There's no way it's catching," Annie said. "He's an old dog. Maybe he's got a tumour or something."

Despite the vet's reassurance that the seizures were due to old age, Dawn was convinced she had contaminated her dog. She had loved Buster too much, loading him with more emotion than an animal can bear. For years he'd witnessed her convulsions. When she woke drowsy and perplexed, dusk having fallen outside, she was aware always of the dog patiently watching her. She wished Mark had the same tolerance. Lately he'd taken to going out before she came to, adding to her disorientation.

At school her epilepsy hadn't been a problem. She felt no shame when she woke with a folded coat under her head and one of her friends a cheerful guard, delighted that Dawn had engineered a diversion from the tedium of the school day.

"He knew about it when we married," she told Annie. "It didn't bother him then. It just happens more frequently now, that's all."

"Men are like that: pathetic," Annie said. "They can't cope with mess. If something nasty needs clearing up, you won't catch them holding the mop and bucket."

So it was inevitable Dawn would spot it in her baby. She knew with complete certainty the first time it happened. Emmie was just a few days old and Dawn couldn't believe that the fluttering life she'd held within her was shelled out and separate. She didn't know where the baby ended and she began. It was a seduction of sorts, the way Emmie moved her with her translucent blondness and petal soft skin. Dawn noticed the delicate tremor that ran across the child's face, so subtle it could be easily missed; the way her grey eyes stared, momentarily emptied; the split second rictus of her peach-down cheeks.

At first the doctor was reassuring. "Babies develop differently. It's too soon to tell."

As weeks went by he was less able to meet Dawn's eyes. Watching his face as obsessively as a lover, she noted every nuance of doubt and evasion, and prepared herself.

At last the doctor said, "I'm worried too. Something doesn't seem quite right. She should be doing more than this now."

Dawn's skin trickled like water. As if to a malediction, her body responded immediately to information her mind had yet to process.

Months passed and there was plenty of information, more than she could bear. The paediatrician spelled out the facts. When no hope remains, no false hope is offered.

"It's a genetic condition related to epilepsy, but different. Have there been other children in the extended family... ?"

Of course there were others, though rarely mentioned. A distant cousin, an aunt long ago, lost their babies. No one knew why. She thought all families were the same. She lay beside the child listening to her soft breathing. Everyone said Emmie looked like her. She had Dawn's eyes: the same colour and shape, embedded to similar depth in their sockets, corneas identically curved. Every cell of Emmie's body had Dawn's mark. As the baby faded something left Dawn like a breath, but slowly, with each day that passed, every milestone not reached, until friends no longer came and Dawn lay on the bed beside the cot and waited. When it happened she knew at first glance. She was ready and there were no tears in her. As the light waned outside she lay motionless until it was so dark there was only an absence of texture and colour.

When Mark returned from work he stared into the cot and his face jerked sideways. He looked at her at last with features she didn't recognise.

"You should have done something."

His voice came from a distance. They were too far apart to comfort each other. She turned on her side away from him. She didn't answer because what the heart knows cannot be spoken — it emerges trite and inarticulate.

The doctor said, "You have to move on. It's been so long."

Every three months her G.P. signed an incapacity certificate. Over time the diagnosis changed from 'bereavement' to 'depression' and finally with nothing said to 'epilepsy', although she'd had seizures all her life and it hadn't prevented her working. She was a nursery assistant for years before Emmie was born, in another life when

16

children were interesting little people, not unbearable reminders of the impotence of love.

Annie said, "Why not try for another baby? It can't happen twice."

Nobody knew that Dawn and her husband lay night after night, chaste in their mutual betrayal and injury. In dreams she made love to the frozen man beside her and woke longing for any touch. She hated every day that came, believing each one separated her further from her child, until she understood: at the moment Emmie stopped breathing, before each cell began its irrevocable unravelling, she was already as far away as it's possible to be.

Five years got behind her as if a day passed. She watched the TV news and in her grief understood things not comprehensible before. Like a wine glass that vibrates to a certain note or cries out as a finger runs along it, her mind resonated to the world's suffering. She saw what nobody else mentioned. Children die in millions every day, their parents mourn and it's commonplace. All she could do was witness, compulsively switching from one news broadcast to the next, so that no death occurred in a corner unnoticed while the world continued its weary business.

Through all the lost time when she only left the house to go to the chemist or doctor, the dog filled spaces in her loneliness. His body was warm like a human being's; his easy presence company. A gate at the end of their garden opened onto a playing field where she let him run free. As Buster loped about the field she felt she was running too. She imagined her feet substantial on the ground, muscles strong, not weedy from years of inactivity. When the wind gusted through the empty nets and barren trees, and the sky descended with the onset of winter dusk, she felt she might fly away unnoticed. Then the dog would return and provide purpose for the next few minutes, grounding her. Sometimes on the deserted playing field she saw a jogger clad in blue and pink, an incongruous humming bird against the bleak grey afternoon. Dawn recognised the woman by her unique and ineffective running style. She ran hunched, her shoulders rotated and forearms uppermost, her legs wheeling outwards from the knees. Her steps were so short she barely seemed to cover ground yet when Dawn looked again she'd completed another dull circuit. Dawn admired her doggedness year after year. Never any faster, never any thinner — surely the longest running and least effective exercise programme in the world.

The dog aged fast after the onset of seizures. He lay by the fire, paws twitching in his sleep. Dawn watched with familiar helplessness, as though time had looped around twice. But the old, tired dog was resigned to weakness. He'd had enough of running. After a few weeks he didn't want to eat.

Annie said, "You've got to let him go."

The vet said, "It's time now. This is the last thing you can do for him."

Annie said, "You could get another dog. I've heard they train special terriers called fit dogs. They watch your face all day for signs, so you can..."

Her voice trailed off, uncertain what to do if warned of an imminent fit. Seeing Annie's eagerness to make things right, Dawn remembered something she'd nearly forgotten about the friendship of women. She saw how funny Annie was, how constant.

She said to help her out, "I'd go somewhere safe. Maybe lie down so I don't hurt myself."

She saw Annie's pleasure that something could be fixed; that life might change and be better for Dawn.

So the vet put down the dog and Dawn stood by the back gate in wellingtons, holding the spade with which she'd buried the stiff body by the hedge. A cold wind howled across the playing field and she watched in distraction the progress of the jogger on her second circuit. Perhaps hoping to compensate for her woeful lack of athletic ability, the woman wore expensive new trainers. Dawn envied the belief that it mattered, that anything mattered: her optimism. The plump jogger scurrying past in posh trainers was such a ludicrous sight she had to smile. The woman immediately stopped, as if she'd waited for this for years, and grinned back.

She said, "What are you doing?"

Dawn said, "I've just buried my dog. I had him put down, he was having fits."

"I'm sorry. That's a shame."

They looked at each other. The woman's eyes creased up like bunched fabric when she smiled, her cheeks were rosy with exertion and her grey hair eccentrically spiked. Dawn saw she was beautiful. And although her old dog had died, she could bear it.

Dawn said, like someone else speaking, "I had a baby once, five years ago. She died when she was eighteen months old."

"I know. I'm sorry," the woman said.

"How do you know?"

19

"Annie at the chemist's told me."

They both laughed because of course Annie knew everything and everybody.

The woman said, "Why don't you come for a run with me?"

"I can't run. I'm really unfit. And I've got these wellies on."

"Come on. You can't go slower than me. It's impossible."

So Dawn leans her fork against the gate and half runs, half walks beside the jogger, whose name is Helen, and who really is very slow. She feels the grass give softly beneath her feet, the air sting and her breath quicken. Looking back at the house she's barely left since Emmie died, she sees how small it is under the sky. And she remembers more about the company of women. You can talk until your jaw aches, and laugh until your stomach hurts and pelvic floor loosens dangerously.

Mark returns from work to a deserted house. The TV playing to itself in the living room tells of another child caught in crossfire. A mother's face is locked in a tetany of grief. Mark dispassionately notes the expression. He no longer remembers how to cry, has forgotten which muscles to use. Knowing the dog was due to die today, his stomach knots tight with dread of the new pit of misery in which he might find his wife. He feels they wander in a wilderness without landmarks, passing the same place again and again. The kitchen door is open and with trepidation he steps into the garden, noting the mound of earth by the hedge. She should have waited for him; she never asks him for anything anymore.

The back gate is swinging and he starts to hurry because he's seen her — he can't believe it — shuffling along in wellingtons on the far side of the field beside that strange jogger. They look so absurd he wants to laugh. There reaches him airborne, like a sound muffled by wind, a sense of something he nearly forgot. As she approaches on the next lap she spots him standing astonished by the gate. Suddenly she's bent double, a gesture he hasn't seen for years, crinkled up with laughter and clutching her belly, helpless. The wind takes away the sound but he hears it in his head like a song remembered.

He stares at Dawn's face: so familiar, so unfamiliar. The lines of middle age have encroached but she's still there, changed yet the same. He holds out his arms.

EVO-STIK AND THE BIGAMIST

My cousin Gary was a bigamist. A trigamist to be precise. Aunty Doris was grandmother to his three families, with a photo collection for each. One set of snaps was usually on display because those children lived nearby. The rest she brought out and rearranged when the others visited. Once from her window my aunty spotted a grandchild heading uninvited towards the tower block entrance. By the time he'd ascended the lift and reached her door, Doris was breathless from her rush to take down and conceal one set of photos, locate and exhibit the next.

As a little girl I would browse around her flat while she bragged of her only son's academic and sporting prowess. Even aged eight, I noticed an inconsistency between the stories and my observations of my loutish teenage cousin. Mum tried to compete, but my top marks in spelling and angelic performance in the nativity play, couldn't compare. Visiting her sister left Mum seething for days.

"You'd think the sun shone out of that boy's arse," she'd say.

The flat smelt of newspapers, Spam and rodent. Gary kept a hamster which he wouldn't let me touch. I'd rejected his conditions for handling the animal as rude. But I loved Doris. Her white hair with nicotine-stained fringe seemed touched with fairy gold. She had an ash tray like a life-sized skull inscribed, *'Poor old Fred, he smoked in bed.'* Each time she stubbed out a fag in Fred's eye socket, I felt a shivery thrill. When my mother left the room, my aunt would pull a biscuit tin from beneath the sofa.

"Quick, Evie. Stuff your face before the boss gets back!"

Mum would return and glare suspiciously at the two of us poring over a puzzle book, while I guiltily tongued claggy traces of custard cream from my palate.

Doris taught me to admire the view from her tower. The high-rise loomed in lordly isolation above a dingy red-brick estate, built to house workers of an industry in mortal decline for decades. We chose to ignore the broken prams and burnt-out sofas on the patchy grass below, and the plastic bags that tossed in the dank wind from the Thames. Instead we exclaimed about the distant twinkling lights of London, and sunsets and rainbows over Dagenham civic centre.

She would regard me thoughtfully and say, "Thank God! At least one of us was spared the hooter."

Doris had an aquiline conk of startling size. My mother bravely suffered the same condition. At adolescence the family curse flowered in the centre of Gary's face. Having inherited a more discreet number from my father, I felt blessed that my cradle had been overlooked by the bad fairy.

Every surface in their living room was packed with knick-knacks. My favourite was a pink and gold cigarette box. When I lifted the lid, a ballerina popped up and pirouetted to the tinny accompaniment of 'Smoke gets in your eyes.'

"You can have that when I'm gone," Doris promised spookily.

One day Gary suggested I open the box. Watching slyly, he urged me to peer up the ballerina's gauzy tutu. Her featureless pink fanny was defaced with male genitals drawn in biro.

"Evo-Stik has got a prick!" said Gary.

I trembled with speechless rage, my dainty alter-ego humiliated as fraud and freak. For years I lacked words for the complexity of this insult. He had composed a song with the same irksome refrain. Hearing this whistled by Gary made my stomach knot tight. At teatime he hummed the ditty beneath his breath until I couldn't eat my share of rabbit-shaped jelly.

"Someone's eyes are bigger than her belly," said my mother.

I lunged sideways and sank my teeth into Gary's bicep. Mum swiped at me with her hankie in consternation.

"Eve! You've made a hole in his jumper! Now say sorry!"

Strands of Doris's hand knitting were stuck to my teeth, but I had tasted Gary's blood.

"The girl's a bundle of nerves," Doris soothed, as my cousin rubbed his arm, smirked and pretended it didn't hurt. "No wonder, when she works so hard at school. It's easier for Gary, he's naturally bright."

After Gary left home I rarely saw him. His room stayed an untouched shrine, the lingerie girls torn from catalogues left abandoned and ageing on the walls. The aroma of hamster lingered. In the ever renewed and shuffled photos on Doris's mantelpiece he featured as an increasingly rotund, complacent family man. His nose loomed from every picture. Each wedding was flashier than the last. The nuptial cars became vintage, the brides younger, the bridesmaids so numerous they resembled a Sunday school outing. Doris never mentioned quarrels or divorces. His used-car business and travels, evidently prosperous, were opaque. The money he borrowed from my father was never returned.

I began to question the legality of Gary's lifestyle. "Gary is an all-round shit," explained my mother. "He'll die roaring. But blood is thicker than water, dear. It wouldn't do to upset Doris."

None of us cared to disillusion Doris. She wasn't naturally cunning, yet to collude with her son's triple life required concentration, dedication and planning. Subsisting on jam sandwiches and syrupy tea, she grew fat. Her legs like two elephant trunks, wrinkled and veiny, were permanently raised on a pouffe. No explanations for her incapacity or estrangement from the outside world were offered. The complexities of her family ties were enough. As if unwilling to complicate her life further, she never left the flat.

As I grew up my dutiful visits to the tower became infrequent. Training to be a social worker at a midlands university, I wrote case studies about dysfunctional families which sounded normal to me. Doris fretted about me living alone so far away, north of Watford where they keep ferrets up their trousers. Worse still, where many of my neighbours were 'foreign'. With new-found professional pomposity, I couldn't let this pass.

"Rubbish!" I rebuked her. "They're the same as people down here."

I waved my thumb at the door to indicate the yobs that lurked on the landing outside. Having bribed them with custard creams not to piss in the hallway, Doris was on cordial terms with them all. Their faces showed every variety and blend of migration to the East End, yet they all spoke the same flat, debased cockney.

"Ah, they're just nippers," she said. "They'll come round!"

The lift and stairs of the tower block had ceased to be mysterious and thrilling, just foetid. The rapid turnover of loitering youths marked the passage of time. Once they were scary big boys, unpredictable as a dog-pack. Primed by Gary, they yelled "Evo-STIK!" behind me on the stairs. For one brief year, pungent with testosterone and hair gel, they'd been strangely alluring. Then, it was, "Evie, hey Evie!" as I sashayed past. Now they were bored, neglected children pretending to be mean, and I was as nameless and inconsequential as the rubbish that accumulated around them.

The flat shrank to a claustrophobic sixties museum piece, the cream and brown floral wallpaper stained yellow as my aunt's dentures. Queasy with jam sandwiches and sweet tea, I'd leave laden with unsuitable gifts from catalogues: soft toys, stiletto shoes, aftershave — all, like my hair and clothes after a visit, reeking of fag smoke. Sometimes to my dismay Doris slipped me a fiver. She saw my feminist dungarees and donkey jacket as pitiful proof that by working for the social, I'd done less well for myself than Gary.

One pre-Christmas visit I found Gary sprawled in Doris's chair, feet on the pouffe, while his mother clattered plates and wheezed joyful songs of homecoming in the kitchen. He nodded at the spread on the tea-table. Doris had done us proud. There were Spam sandwiches, biscuits thickly spread with butter, and the remains of a rabbit-shaped jelly doused in evaporated milk. He'd eaten the head and ears and left me the rump.

"Help yourself, Evo. It's been years, I'd forgotten you!"

This wasn't true. He'd heard enough to decide my life had failed, and felt compelled to present me with the evidence — my exile up north, pittance of a salary and woeful inability to catch a man.

"It's all about presentation," he advised.

He pulled a photo of a brassy bimbo from his wallet and gazed at her fondly. On the mantelpiece a different, older, trollop grinned down in wedding dress and false eyelashes. His shell-suit crackled as he leaned forward and tugged the bib of my dungarees.

"You should keep in better nick, girl. Get a makeover. Lipstick, hairdo, all that. I reckon you'd scrub up nicely if you tried."

He leaned back yawning and spread thick thighs to reveal the sleeping-ferret outline of his crotch.

"Unless you're not bothered about blokes these days. Social workers and all that. Feminists. You know."

Gary actually leered.

The last time I saw Doris, she smirked as she handed me an Eiffel Tower in a plastic globe, shaking it to demonstrate the snow storm. She'd been on a day trip to France. If the ravens had left the Tower of London I'd have been less astonished.

"I just woke up and thought, sod it girl, you've never seen Paris. Let's go!" she said.

She'd taken years of pension money from a hidden biscuit tin, called a taxi and instructed the startled driver to take her to Dover, across the channel on the ferry and then to Paris. She bought postcards and drove round all the sights — 'gallivanting' — and downed a bottle of French red in the cab on the way home, pushing the cork in with her thumbs. She was jubilant, smug, and determined never to leave the flat again.

"Next time they'll have to take me out of here in a box!"

Not long after, the curse of Fred the skull did my aunty in. I heard the news with disbelief and vague self reproach. Mum wept into her gin and blamed Gary for her sister's untimely death at the age of eighty four.

"She should have drowned the kid at birth. I knew the strain would catch up with her in the end. And now he's phoned to say he can't get home before the funeral. He's in Turkey, or is it Turkestan? He wants me to organise everything. He goes, 'I trust you to be discreet, Aunty. Know what I mean?' But it's so complicated, Evie. I can't think straight. Will you sort it out for me, dear?"

She pushed Doris's address book towards me.

"No problem, Mum," I said.

As I pocketed the book, the reek of fag smoke made me want to howl.

"I'm all alone now," my mother cried inaccurately, helping herself to another triple slug of gin. "The last of the line!"

I arrived first at the flat to get things ready. As I puffed up ten flights because the lift was broken, I imagined my auntie's final trip down. I could almost hear her wheezy "Heh, heh, heh!" as she embroidered it into an anecdote: hunky men exclaiming "Oo er, missus!" at her bloomers as they crammed her in the box; her nose tapping like a woodpecker with every step as they heaved it downstairs.

28

Without Doris, the air in the flat seemed thinner. The dense fog that had further delayed Gary's flight pressed at the window. I admired the spread I'd prepared earlier. She would have been proud of the rabbit jellies, evaporated milk served in a Toby jug and custard creams dainty on a doily. The Evo-Stik song ran through my head and for the first time made me smile.

When the guests arrived I circulated with a bottle of cheap white, noting the cruelly random distribution of the family hooter, and eavesdropped on the introductions. Then I moved to the hall to witness my cousin's belated entrance. Sombre and stuffed in his expensive suit, Gary shook my hand and gravely accepted my condolences. Waving his arms grandly he suggested I take anything, anything at all, as a memento. I'd already found the piles of half completed puzzle books, rows of dusty knick-knacks, and Fred. The bathroom contained denture fixative and a doll with crinoline skirts concealing the toilet roll. The ballerina box and pension tin had disappeared.

My mother, well into her cups, fell upon him weeping about the last in the line. As he detached himself and entered the living room, I thought I'd never seen anyone turn such a clammy, gratifying grey.

"Blood is thicker than water and all that, Gaz," I said.

Of course it isn't. I'd known since I gnawed through his jumper and drew blood — the one violent act of my pacifist life. He stared at me glassily. Filling his tumbler, I let a little wine slop onto his shirt.

Huddled in a corner, three women muttered urgently. With their stilettos, peroxide streaks and clunky jewellery, they looked like sisters. On the sofa Gary's six children, aged five to twenty five, sat together for the first time, the youngest on the eldest's knee. There were three photo albums in front of them and they were studying every page. A bead of sweat rolled slowly down my cousin's nose. I watched its long journey, fascinated.

I said, "There's one good thing about a funeral, Gaz. It brings the family together."

Gary moved, as if to the door. I caught his sleeve and held fast.

THERESA'S SPEAR

We care for Beatrice like the baby none of us had. She's sweeter, more placid than an infant; she always was. Her smile's the same, though her mind is hidden behind steamed glass. She still knows me. When we were young the affection and fervour stored inside us had to find expression somehow. We didn't know why we were kept apart. Or why in the end Mother Superior took me aside.

"Theresa, our mission in Africa needs you. You must go soon. God is calling you."

For years I talked to Beatrice in my head. I whittled every conversation we'd had, shaving off meaning curl by curl. I couldn't say why I woke in tears, or what I missed. The answer I knew lay in words. But what use were they when for weeks before I left for the mission, she would neither speak nor listen?

Except to say, "I've been praying. It's a sin."

A swift, sharp twisting in the throat.

When I returned to the convent years later, before she became ill, we spoke of that time. I learned that many of my letters had been kept from her. Pages were removed, their intensity censored. Did Mother Superior know what she was doing? She believed attachments would distract us from our calling. But what else remains? Like the tenderness I feel for her frail body. All that's left of my Beatrice now.

The mission was a scattering of mud brick, whitewashed buildings outside a village: a small clinic, church, library and guest room. Each woman had a thatched round hut. I picked up the language fast, aided by the two local nuns. Chichewa isn't difficult, with seven words for washing, but none for the emotions that sluiced through me as I quietly performed my litany of duties. My dreams in the new language were serene, not played out hopelessly.

We trained novices, a stream of young women through the years, most barely more than children. But they were mothers too, or soon became so. They'd leave the mission one weekend and come back married on Monday. Months later they'd briefly disappear again, returning with a baby strapped on the back. It didn't matter. No one came to see. Mother Superior's fierce definition of sin was as meaningless here as the Christmas card of a white, plump baby Jesus she sent the mission every year.

"Sister, I stole sugar from the shop."

"Sister, I had sex with a man for money."

The novices told me everything. Not in confessional, but at my wooden table with a bottle of Fanta and two chipped glasses between us. At first I resisted. Yet they worked so hard in the fields before lessons, and worried so much about their children. I knew it was incorrect, but I absolved them.

"Say a prayer when you pass the shop."

"Don't see that man again. He's no good for you."

In the absence of a priest, I gave negligible penances.

Four-wheel drives sometimes pulled up at the village shop. Huge, pink tourists got out, hunting for beer. They dithered, baffled by the empty shelves, while children twittered like flycatchers around them. And for a few years we had a regular visitor, Ian, the young aid agency doctor from the district hospital three miles away. He came in the Land Rover the first time, bumping up the red dirt road with dogs and children galloping beside, to ask if our clinic might be used as a vaccination station. We had no fridge, but vaccines stay cold for an afternoon in a clay pot of water. New to Malawi, he looked around the clinic anxiously.

"There's nothing here."

I showed him sheets cut in strips and neatly edged to make bandages; needles and razorblades boiled and stored in disinfectant; bottles of gentian violet. The concrete floor was swept and scrubbed daily.

"It's enough."

It wasn't, but I'd grown used to scarcity.

Later Ian would visit on Sunday afternoons, cycling beside the railway track to arrive unannounced. He talked of his work and self doubt, the pain and poverty all around. Fifteen years younger, more hopeful than I, he foresaw change and improvement. His words slid little points of meaning into my mind. He borrowed from our library, ransacking the mildewed cartons of donated books that I was taking years to unpack. We marvelled at the titles that end up in a mission, bequeathed from the estates of dead men far away. He drank tea and ate peanuts at my table, and gave me his delicate ink drawings to brighten my walls. My room felt empty when he went. I'd seek out Blessings, the little boy who spent most afternoons in the shade thrown by my hut, and scoop him into my lap.

The mission was full of children. Village kids darted around, rolled through my room, or sat in a staring solemn line while I read. So many, they became one hilarious, tumbling child. They dressed in absurd rags — an old bra

33

belted round the waist, a pair of bloomers worn like a blouse. Their names bizarre: Fatness, Trouble, Mattress. The nuns suggested more fitting ones — Mary, Peter, Margaret — but none stuck. Childhood was pitifully short. By age six or seven they carried water in tin cans on their heads and scraped the soil beside their mothers. But no child touched me like Blessings. He was quieter, more watchful, than the others. Whenever I sat down he climbed onto my lap. I fretted over his dull skin and the orange patches in his hair. His destitute mother came and went from the village on desperate errands, staying away for weeks. She knew we would feed him in her absence. Some nights I woke to find Blessing's hard little body tucked under my arm.

One Sunday afternoon Ian and I were drinking tea and discussing books when an excited bunch of children ran towards us.

"Sister, come quickly!"

Blessings lay curled in the shade of a mango tree. He'd been there all morning. I'd assumed he was asleep. Now I saw his chest heave with each breath; the skin between his ribs suck in and out; his glazed eyes. I pulled down one hot, dry eyelid and recognised the sick pallor of malaria.

"Help me get a drip up," Ian said.

He took a needle from his pocket and tried to insert it into Blessing's tiny arm, but the veins had shrunk beneath his skin. The child lay crucified. He didn't flinch or cry out as the point went in again and again. Ian lacerated the little boy's arms and legs, cutting down with a razor blade to find a deep vein. The children watched silently. I pushed the doctor away and sealed my mouth over Blessing's, tasting apple-like sweat and acrid vomit as I tried to blow back his life. I couldn't stop. His chest rose and fell with mine, while the sun poured down on us its white, empty light.

"Theresa, leave him now. It's futile."

Ian held my arm as we looked at Blessing's body in the dust beneath the mango tree. Children sobbed and hugged each other and darted forward to touch his cooling skin. Mothers ran keening, each desperate that the dead child not be theirs. The doctor's hand trembled and I knew he was right. There was no point, none at all.

Weeks passed then while I did little but farm. Abandoning my habit for tee shirt and chitenje, I hacked at the ground to plant next year's maize. Without my veil the sun's hands pressed me down into the earth. I yearned for Beatrice. Blessing's mother returned and I led her to the little heap of soil strewn with jacaranda blossom. I hugged her awkwardly, both of us dry eyed, and murmured words of comfort I no longer believed.

Unaware that I'd changed, the novices still came to my hut for tea and confession. Their sins were nothing, irrelevant frailties, compared with the monstrous injustices they suffered.

I said, "If you sleep with him, get him to use something."

"But Sister, it's not allowed!"

"It's different here. You're allowed to keep safe. You have to look after yourself."

Then someone began to fill the God-shaped hole in my heart: Ian, my friend. An impossible, foolish longing snarled my days and nights. For the first time in years I studied myself in a mirror. As a young woman I was vain. There were few mirrors in the convent, but when I polished

the one in the guest room my eyes slipped like fish to find
their reflection. Mother Superior's stern lecture on pride
left me sobbing, and ever after when I cleaned glass I
watched my hand, not my face. Now I held the oil lamp to
my smeared image. I saw eyes in grey craters, cheekbones
like dark triangles — a gaunt, lined face. Ian had a lover, a
beautiful young local woman, a nurse I supposed. He never
spoke of her, perhaps assuming I'd disapprove. I saw her
once in the market. One of the girls, laughing, pointed her
out though I pretended I wasn't interested in gossip.

Our Sunday conversations enclosed a new pain. He
never guessed, I'm certain. If I weakened and my eyes
searched his, I'd look away, get up and move about the
room. Sometimes he regarded me curiously.

"Are you all right, Theresa? You don't seem yourself."

A professed atheist, he was shocked when I admitted
what I'd lost.

"But you've seen so many children die before Blessings.
We did what we could. You're burnt out, you've been here
so long. Maybe you should go home for a bit, have a
break."

I considered the convent, my home. Mother Superior
had long since died. Her replacement I heard was younger,
kinder, more accepting of foibles. I remembered the cool
high rooms and marble floor corridors; the clean grey
morning light; the ageing good tempered nuns, my friends.
Haltingly I spoke of Beatrice.

Ian said, "Young girls get intense like that. It's natural."

For this I was exiled. Beatrice, Blessings, Ian. So much
love misplaced and wasted. How could it be natural?

"Go home and see Beatrice, I'm sure she misses you. You're a good person you know, Theresa. The best I ever met."

Ian reached out and held my arm as he had that day under the mango tree.

That was all. And maybe it was enough.

NASMA'S MALADY

From time to time something happens to me. There's a thinning, a delicate disruption, where my skin touches air. Boundaries blur until I no longer know where I end and other people begin. My mind is capsized by the thoughts of others. Crowds confuse me because I can't hear myself think. This feeling may vanish after a few seconds or last all day.

It wasn't always so. These bouts began, like the menopause, because it was time. At first I mistook the hot slide on my skin as illness. But I knew something had changed when the radio by the bed began to broadcast news I could feel. A flaw from outside had entered me. Listening to reports of a plane crash, I feel myself fall from the sky. Suicide bombs come nearer until they explode inside my chest. The anguish of dying mothers and lost children overwhelms me. During these times I can't distance myself from suffering — it buries me.

Outside I feel better. I can breathe. Night falls early at this time of year but I'm never frightened. A middle-aged woman in a shabby coat attracts no attention in a city. And nothing can happen that hasn't already happened. Nothing can be taken I haven't already lost.

I know the shape of every hour that passes on these streets. In January by five o'clock children have returned from school and most people are bolted inside their houses. Shutters blind the shop windows. The health centre remains open but patients in the waiting room are uneasy. They'd rather be home, away from the darkness.

They shuffle their problems — headaches that come and go, breathing difficulties — so the doctor will understand. When I pass the surgery other people's symptoms jangle in my head.

By seven o'clock there's a different feeling on the street, a change of air. Shadows thicken beyond pools of streetlight. Boys too old for PlayStations clutter the off-license door. Around them slide the sharper, denser shapes of teenage gangs. Voices suspended in mist erupt in laughter or rage. I slip past and they barely notice me. A hum, a tension, passes across my shoulders and down my arms. For a second I feel their hostilities and longings. Then I pull free and only the wind blows through me.

At eight the doctor leaves the surgery, rolling a shutter down over the door. All day his liturgy of duties wards off sadness. Now as I pass unseen, his troubled thoughts open inside me like flowers. He believes his wife no longer loves him. Perhaps she'll leave. Her eyes meet his with a new, calm withholding of expression. He knows the man, pictures them together. Sometimes it's too much: his wife, the procession of anguished stories he hears — how can he contain it? All day he talks to people washed up from anywhere. Questions he can't ask hang like bubbles in air.

Why are you here? What happened to you?

Instead he says, "What sort of pain? How do you sleep at night?"

Sometimes I go to see him. When I described my malady he listened. He's a good man, he tries, but has heard nothing like it.

He said, "Nasma, women of your age. Your life has been difficult, sometimes the mind play tricks. You don't get enough sleep. I'm worried about you."

39

Some nights I sleep, but fever wakes me. I crawl onto Amos like a raft. His arms encircle me and his penis stirs slightly in his sleep. I want to melt into the surface of his skin. But the attacks are too strong. There's a sadness that's not my own, and whispering voices. I have to get out.

Our terraced house opens onto the street. Outside the front door is a gutted car. I've lived here eight years but know my neighbours only by sight. Many of the original elderly inhabitants have died. I recognise a pattern. An old person stops going out, the house is empty, then re-occupied. A hurricane sweeps up people from all over the world and drops them on Poppy Street. It's as good as anywhere. Scattered like salt, we don't understand each other. Our half-greetings are wary.

Nobody asks, *Why are you here? What happened to you?*

We wait for something to happen. For life to regain meaning, or for hope enough to reinvent it.

This condition of mine is recent, no more than a year old. I've yet to discover whether it's infirmity or power. When I arrived in this country I was ordinary, defenceless. Less than that: nothing. At the immigration desk I rolled up my sleeves to show my arms and hands. Not my flesh — surely someone else's? The uniformed woman was shocked. Her eyes flicked to mine as I was led away. A doctor examined me, then a lawyer. Not everyone is given shelter. I'm grateful, I don't forget.

For years I couldn't believe my luck. I was safe. Those men with mouths twisted like wire couldn't reach me. I believed I'd got away. And if I waited long enough Hasim would escape too. The hurricane would fling him down in Poppy Street. He was with me all the time, even in dreams.

40

In my thoughts I talked to him constantly, referred everything to him. If I flirted a little with someone, I imagined him jealous. I went to college, worked hard to learn English. Looking back I can't believe I was so optimistic, elated even — perhaps a little mad. Sometimes I glimpsed the prison: a dark corner; a flick of anger that disappeared into somebody's eye; shouts on the street. And in nightmares, so I learned not to sleep. My body and face became softer, middle-aged. I didn't mind, it was safer that way. Hasim would recognise me.

For a while my old life — as teacher, rich woman and Hasim's wife — felt like a dream. My memories, of conversations mostly, felt surreal. I used to be garrulous; friends and colleagues teased that I never shut up. Hasim and I talked all the time. Here, closed on myself like a folding chair, I rarely speak. When my English was good enough I found a job on a supermarket till. Nobody asked where I came from or why I was here. I couldn't believe people with access to information were so ignorant. I met Amos stacking boxes in the storeroom. But my spurious confidence was beginning to slip. The memories I evaded were catching up and would soon overtake me. I began to see things, delicate as a hair on a lens, in shadows and at night. Then all at once it was upon me. Heart racing, sweating, flooded by fear, I remembered everything. Had I really forgotten? Again and again, in scarlet explosions, those men came back.

And like damp through a wall seeped the cold certainty that Hasim was dead.

I clung to Amos then. Tall and slow moving, he asks little of me. He walks as if on crumbling ground, one careful step at a time. His English is poor and we've no words to bind us. He traces my scars with his fingers, but says nothing. His back is deeply gouged by knife or machete. *Why are you here? What happened to you?* I've never asked. His massive male presence surrounds me, fills doorways, blocks light from windows like a sandbag. Amos would stop them. He would protect me.

Hasim's wrists were thin like mine. He wept as they pushed us into different cars.

Amos whimpers in his sleep but I never wake him. I don't want nightmares to leach into his day. When headlights sweep the window or there's sudden noise outside, sweat pours from him and I smell Africa on his skin. I watch over him, this stranger, uncertain who's stronger. When I return from my night walks he's awake and waiting, fearful as a child. I let his body engulf mine. We've no other way to calm each other.

My life now is a book bent back along its spine. Two broken halves. Every moment two moments — before and after my arrest. I'm not a brave woman. I gave them everything, did what they said, told all I knew. When they'd taken all I had, they let me go and I boarded a plane. But I brought the prison with me. Many times an hour I'm there. Triggered by a colour, a smell, a movement: cascades of connecting images I've learned to step round. The present is lost — a pause, a missed heartbeat — as I keep the days going. And always I'm vigilant. I never sleep long.

Midnight. As I open the front door streetlight pours into the hall, sudden and scouring. The turbulence inside me is cold as the skin of frost on the pavement. I pass thin boys with drugged eyes flat as ironed sheets. At the hospital gates I turn and walk back past the mosque. Later there will be the call to prayer. Elderly men will leave their houses in flimsy footwear. Few believe they'll stay long enough in this cold country to make use of a stout pair of shoes, or accept, even after thirty years, that a temporary situation has become permanent.

I'll stay until Hasim comes. Where else in this big cooling world could he find me? If I walk far enough and check every face I'll recover him: my darling, my true love. Eight years have passed since the police took him away, but I'll know him. I spot him sometimes in a retreating back or turned head. Once, outside the mosque in religious dress. My atheist husband, I had to smile — are you really so changed? But close up just a boy, not like my Hasim at all.

One o'clock. I'm tired now, sick with the thoughts of others. Seeking solace, meaning, in other minds, I find only tracks in snow that loop and vanish. I don't know the reason for this malady, or the good of it. One day it will become clear. But now I must hurry home. Amos needs me. He can't be left alone too long.

EYE OF THE STORM

Meek and lost behind spectacles, the dentist's eyes
won't lock onto mine. They slide in one direction, his words
in another. It's unnerving.
"Really, there's no need to panic," he says.
I don't accept I panicked. Gurgled a little, maybe.
"Try to stay calm. It will only take five minutes."
A daddy-long-legs dances, seventies style, across a
digital clock on the wall. 2:16 — by 2:21 this will be over.
Dislocated sound pours from a radio. The dentist's gloved
hands are inside my mouth, insistent.

2:17. Lignocaine creeps through my jaw. Air begins to
leak from the room, bit by bit. Flying litter bumps against
the glazed window of the surgery. The wind has trailed me
all summer. Moaning down the canyons of concrete it
followed me here, whipping my legs. I no longer buy
newspapers, but glimpse headlines in shops or over
shoulders: high winds circle the earth; hurricanes trash far
away countries; people are blown away.
At night, storms hunt across the moon.
Standing at the window of my flat I watched the
bulldozers and diggers move like aliens towards us.
Everything has been cleared away, block after block taken
down, our building the last. Three residents, old and batty,
refused to be re-housed. The council hopes they'll die
before eviction notices are served. We stay too, not in
defiance or solidarity, but through inertia. Piece by piece
I've packed our possessions into cardboard boxes, taken

down pictures and wrapped crockery in newspaper. We live frugally like saints, one cup and plate each, waiting for something to happen. Twenty years in one place should roar as I pick it apart, but disintegrates in my fingers like damp paper. Only my son's room is undisturbed. When I open his door and suggest he starts to pack, he stares with affronted blankness from a sweet haze of cannabis smoke. He knows he should have strong feelings about the move, but they escape him.

2:18. Stopping my mouth with metal instruments, the dentist murmurs something about a squirrel he feeds in his garden. Unable to reply, I reflect I haven't seen squirrel, cat, or any living thing for some time. I hang nuts from my balcony but no birds come. The last tree was cut down a month ago. The buzz of the drill inside my head reminds me of the electrical saws that took the tree apart — I felt my skin vibrate even through closed windows. Severed limbs screeched as they fell. As they dug out the roots with mechanical diggers, the thump-thump jarred my aching tooth.

My eyes have yet to adjust to the gaps left by the tree and the demolished buildings. I still see them, ghost images, behind my eyelids. Losing my mother was like that.

Agnes, the most nimble of the remaining residents, was on the stairs this morning carrying a cardboard box full of rubbish. I watched her trail backwards and forwards, lug stuff to the tree stump hole and chuck it in. She must be clearing her flat after all. I'd assumed her to be as trenchant as the other two. There are years left yet in the old girl's body, if not her brain; her legs, although dubiously stained, still muscular. She smells now — she never used to — and her grey socks are tangled around her ankles.

"Shame about the tree," I remarked, trying to help with a box.

Agnes swatted me away. "Good riddance, more like. Bloody trees. Suck the goodness out of the air. Can't breathe these days."

She talks like a swimmer breathing. Cigarette smoke creeps up her face to get lost in her hair.

The bulldozers haven't returned for weeks. All is quiet now while they wait for the old people to die.

2:20. The dentist rocks backwards and forwards inside my mouth. My head lurches as if with powerful alcohol. One night there was an earthquake: a small one. Empty clothes hangers jangled inside the wardrobe. I thought the diggers were working again. Greg stirred beside me as the streetlight outside flickered and dropped blocks of yellow light on his creased monkey-like face. In the morning he remembered nothing but it was in the papers: 'Small earthquake shakes city, Richter scale 3.' Nothing to get excited about.

My nerves are peeled. Never have I felt so short-tempered, so full of aches and unease. I mentioned it to the doctor when I consulted him about my swollen face. Taking a chart from his drawer he asked questions, ticking boxes as I replied.

"Your scores show you are moderately anxious and depressed," he announced, pushing the sheet towards me as proof.

His impassivity prickled me. I imagined him perched on his bed in button-up pyjamas, ticking a questionnaire. "Your scores show you are moderately sexually repelled and seriously irritated with me," he tells his tautly smiling wife.

"Actually I think I've got cancer, in the jaw or stomach or somewhere."

The words are comfort. They make sense of the foreboding that has dogged me all summer.

"Like my mother," I reminded him.

The last time I'd seen him was at my mother's bedside a year before. A lifelong hypochondriac, she nonetheless omitted to tell either of us about her stomach pains. On her regular visits to surgery she carefully laid a disappearing trail of irrelevant symptoms. As her flesh melted she claimed to be slimming, until she was in bed, a yellow skeleton, too frail to stand but refusing hospital admission because there was nothing wrong with her. The doctor stood stiff and dismayed while I berated him and my mother vomited her life's blood into a bucket. And all the time we argued and she deteriorated, she was receiving texts from a medium.

"Mother, you don't even believe that rubbish. And when did you learn to text?"

The medium said the people my mother could see packing the room were my father and grandparents come to take her home. My mother slid out of consciousness while the doctor fiddled with needles and drips. He gave up at last because it was too late. Another text came, which I didn't read.

How can anyone so vibrantly infuriating as my mother, be dead?

2:21 has come and gone. The dentist lied, it isn't finished yet. He adjusts his position. The nurse hoovers neatly inside my mouth, sucking up bloody fountains of spittle. All summer an abscess has been forming on the root of my tooth. Maybe that's what was wrong with me, all along: the body's shocked response to infection, rallying white cells and discharging chemicals. Irritation seeps like toxin though my blood stream. No one escapes. Not Simon, my slothful son, nor Gabrielle, my gormlessly holy daughter, and certainly not Greg, my plug-ugly husband, hiding his wobbly teeth behind his hand.

"I've got dental phobia," he says.

"You're not phobic. You're just scared."

I find his teeth sometimes. He hides them like an alcoholic's bottles, behind the alarm clock or under toilet rolls. Once, in my slippers. As the house empties he has fewer hiding places. I wonder how long before all his teeth are gone. Already he's grotesque as a cartoon tramp. He sneezes and I see him secrete an expelled tooth in his tissue; later I find it in my underwear draw. He thinks if he doesn't smile I won't notice. I trick him by talking about Gabrielle, rocking in the arms of Jesus on a missionary ship off the coast of South America. Whenever our daughter is mentioned, his face forms dopey indulgent folds and he forgets to cover his mouth.

"Don't you pity those South Americans?" I say. "She must be getting on their nerves very badly by now. If she wants to do good to heathens, there's more in this city than there. Probably more in these flats."

"Oh, I don't know," he mumbles. "I think we're quite a spiritual lot. Sort of in touch with the cosmos."

"Who are you talking about?" I snap. "Three mad old women, an idiot boy and a brain-fried old hippy? And don't you dare suggest I'm in touch with anything. Don't even think about it."

"You're proud of her really," he says. "Her eyes shine with sincerity."

"They bulge," I correct him. "She only does it to wind me up. She was always the same. Hanging round my legs when I was trying to get rid of Jehovah's Witnesses. Smirking at them. She'd tell them she wanted to go to Sunday school, but her mother wouldn't let her."

"I think she does a lot of good," he says.

"But there are hurricanes in South America, landslides, mudslides. Those poor people have enough to put up with and anyway, it's not safe. Watch the news — everything's getting closer. Look outside — the estate is disappearing. I had to jump over a crack like a chasm on the way to book my appointment with the dentist. Have you been into the city centre lately? All the trees have blown down, squashing the cars. There's hardly any traffic left. Everyone is leaving but us."

2:35. Soon ten minutes will have elapsed. I smell the dentist's deodorant and beneath that his armpit, which pumps up and down not far from my face. He continues to blather about squirrels. I wonder where he lives. Maybe somewhere in this city there's a better place where trees still stand. How does he get to work now his surgery is a lone building in a wasteland of rubble? Where does he cross the cracks?

Perhaps it's just my age, as my mother always said. Exasperation at the memory hurls itself on nothing.

Sometimes I spot it in the mirror: old age, waving cockroach feelers from a keyhole, gone before you believe what you've seen. With the passage of time my mother's face thickens like a skin over mine. But I don't accept it. I feel the same, jumpy as a hamster inside my baggy pelt. The old people in our flats think I'm young, a baby. When we moved in I was pregnant and they were already old; now they are ancient, dusty things. For years I've received a few pounds every month from social services to look after them. At first I shopped and tidied, but as time passed my duties became more personal. These days I empty commodes and scrub false teeth. When the bulldozers came, two of the old women took to their beds. Communicating with each other by text, they plot against the council. What's with all this texting? How did people so decrepit learn such a skill?

"They can't carry us out in our beds," they say. "It would look bad in the papers."

"When did you last see a paper?" I say. "They've changed. Something is happening and we haven't been told. The council won't come, they've forgotten us. I haven't seen a child for months. I think they've all been evacuated."

One more wrench, something crunches, and the tooth is out. 2:38. Twelve minutes, start to finish. The dentist shyly waves the tooth, an antique peg — surely not mine? I stare in disbelief. How did it get so old? Spitting blood into the sink I feel lighter, purged, with a gap in my head where a tooth should be.

The dentist says, "That's the last one I'll be doing."

He doesn't charge me anything.

I walk home on wobbly legs. The wind has dropped. Plastic bags and strangely, sheep's wool are stuck all over the barbed wire around the demolition sites. Everything but our block is razed to the ground. Most of the windows are boarded up. Only ours shows a sliver of light.

We don't bother lock the door anymore and it swings open at my touch. The flat throbs with music. An old hippy anthem, 'Free bird', is playing and my son and husband are dancing in each other arms. At last, Simon has piled up boxes outside his room. The living room furniture has been pushed against the walls. I sink to the floor and watch my family critically.

"I think it's the end of the world," I say.

In the din my voice goes out like a match.

The music changes pace. The men twitch around the room, strumming hard on imaginary guitars. Greg leaps, Mick Jagger style, into the air and as his feet hit the ground a tooth patters onto the carpet. He stares at it forlornly.

"All this hippy stuff is just a con," I shout. "A cover-up for drink and dope and something wrong inside your head."

He grabs my hand and pulls me to him, fitting his roomy mouth around my ear.

"You never thought you'd end up with a troll, doll," he says.

"No, it wasn't supposed to be like this. And where's Gabrielle? Why is she so far away? Hasn't she heard of texting?"

"She's fine," he says. "Everything's fine. You've had a tooth out, you're shocked. You'll feel better in the morning. And we'll be leaving here soon. It won't be long now, we're ready."

Letting myself go loose in his arms I cry for my tooth and my lost mother, and a world I don't understand any more.

Later in bed Greg takes my hand, holds it to his lips and goes to sleep. For the first time in months there's no pain in my jaw. Perhaps I'll be able to sleep now. Outside, the wind has dropped and a blackbird is calling. I think of the dentist feeding the last squirrel in the city, and my three old ladies scheming. I imagine Gabrielle on her missionary ship, rolling unperturbed in the eye of a storm. In her arms, no doubt, some toothy God-botherer she has seduced with her pop-eyed piety and goofy gospel songs, the hussy.

I wish for my daughter someone to love her until the last tooth drops from her head.

I dream her a world without end.

THE ALPHABET DIET

"Congratulations Mick," says the nurse. "You're not morbidly obese anymore."

"So what am I?" I ask.

Her eyes, quick fish in a fine net, slip towards me then back to the computer screen.

"Obese."

"Oh," I say.

"It's brilliant! You've done really well. What's on the menu this week?"

"Kippers, Kit-Kats and kiwi fruit."

"Weird. And next week?"

"Lamb chops, legumes and lettuce," I say.

"It's an odd diet. Maybe you should discuss it with the doctor. But if it works for you, he'll be pleased. This surgery has the heaviest patients in the city."

I stand up so she can stretch a tape measure round my waist. For a moment I imagine she's embracing me. I've never smelt a woman's hair without paying.

"How do you know that?" I ask.

"Pooled data," she replies, mysteriously. "We also have the most cases of depression."

"Maybe it's the long wait in the waiting room," I say. "People get fat and miserable sitting there for hours. You should make the doors narrower to keep us all out."

She presses keys. On the screen a graph of my body mass index trails gratifyingly downwards.

"What happens when my body mass index hits zero?" I ask.

"We'll cross that bridge when we come to it."

I run at night. A fat man jogging is conspicuous in the day. I don't need an alarm clock. I wake naturally, with a jerk, at three — a time without perspective or reason, when shadows from outside break in and enter me with deep, levering grief. It's better to be up and out of the house. Downstairs, cold light from the TV flickers across my father's face. His eyes are glassy with fatigue, but at least he's distracted from himself. Far worse are the nights when he wanders from room to room, stray words of loss and longing escaping from a recess in his mind that he's ashamed for me to see.

Running at night I'm invisible. Only the security lights that switch on and off as I pass mark my existence. A yellow mist hugs the streetlights. In the deserted park someone has scattered broken glass at the foot of the slide and twisted the swing seats too high for a child to reach. A stitch makes me walk for a while. Frost crunches beneath my trainers like snail shells. In the day I avoid the park because I know that a lone fat man is not allowed near children.

Returning home I find my father at last asleep in his chair, his face, creased like linen, supported by one hand. I slide my arm under his.

"Come on, Dad. Bedtime."

He leans against me. "You're wasting away, son."

"Rubbish. I'm just slimming."

I handle him gently, like a fragile crawling creature that might shed a leg. Pushing his bedroom door open with my shoulder, I guide him to the bed. Every surface and the floor are heaped with incongruous items: magazines in

54

unopened plastic covers, ancient packets of biscuits, kitchen implements, toys. I frisk his pockets for the day's shoplifted spoils — six teaspoons and a bottle of Kahlua.

The night recedes and in another hour it will be dawn. My father will sleep now. I fry a kipper and eat slowly, trying to imagine something else, but defeated by its inalienable fishiness. These days food fantasies move around my head like shapes in fog. I dream of feasts, and ordinary things like cornflakes, sandwiches and apples. My mouth tastes of metal and my pores emit a sharp, unfamiliar odour which I disguise with deodorant. It's alarmingly easy to lose stone after stone. I'm unwrapping. As each layer is stripped away I fear what may be exposed, but when the final packing has gone I suspect there'll be nothing inside at all.

Although it's only seven when I get to the shop, Gavin is there. The bucket of sand by the back door is littered with fag ends. *Blue Lizard Computers*. My shop's logo, which I designed, fills me with ambivalence. I never expected that at forty two years old I would own a computer repair shop and live with my father. But then, I had few expectations. Customers see an immaculate white area with laminated notices, but behind the counter Gavin and I spend our days in a nicotine stained backroom among piles of computer towers.

"Rabbit woman was back," he says. "Bloody thing fused the motherboard again. Second time this month."

He shows me a cable, nibbled neatly in two by rodent teeth. There's something wrong with Gavin. His eyes slide and fix at chin level. When I'm out he searches customers' files for salacious material as if rummaging through a lingerie drawer. I'm astonished that porn is left so trustingly on hard drives — perhaps people see us as monks in our austere cell. I won't look at the images he unearths. Pictures of women splayed out and poked about dismay me. Even page three girls make me uncomfortable.

But then, I know nothing. My sexual encounters can be counted on the fingers of one hand. They replay like worn videos behind my eyelids before sleep. I embellish them not with lurid detail, but tenderness — a woman's fingers in my hair, her hand on my cheek. At other times I don't let myself remember. A cyst of shame encloses the reality: lumbering, sweaty acts in dingy rooms; drugged women with eyes empty as water. I could never get my clothes back on fast enough. Once I asked a woman to kiss me on the lips, and saw the disgust that until then she'd managed to conceal.

During lulls in the day's work Gavin trawls news sites for articles on large blubbery animals. He pins the printouts on the wall, our only joke. I'm interested in both stories he found today. Moscow is so cold this winter that the zoo has decided to give the elephants vodka from buckets. I imagine them staggering about, huge and plastered. Then there's a whale that got lost and swam up the river Thames. Expecting something akin to a submarine, I'm disappointed that the creature in the photo is so small, an insignificant fishy thing winched onto a barge to die. Perhaps deprived of plankton it lost not just its way, but itself. Maybe its body mass index shrank to zero.

Body mass index 29. The nurse is delighted.

"Great stuff! You're now merely overweight. What is it this week?"

"Sausages, satsumas, sweet potatoes," I say.

"How vile."

As she wraps the blood pressure cuff around my arm I ask, "What do you think of speed dating?"

"Not my scene. Aren't you a bit shy for it?"

"I could be good. You only have to speak for five minutes. I've prepared a short talk on large mammals."

"You'll slay them."

I wait until she turns to the screen before I say, "I wouldn't know what to do with an ordinary woman."

"Nonsense. It's time you had a girlfriend, Mick."

An hour after the speed date session I sit beside Irena in the pub, dazed and dizzy at the pace of it all. She's tiny, late thirties and exhausted. Her eyes lie in dark saucers of bone. If I had a type, she wouldn't be it. Her rapid speech and eastern European accent are baffling, but like difficult music, become clearer.

"Why aren't you married?" she asks.

"No one would have me. I'm too fat."

She looks surprised. "You're not fat."

The conversation moves so fast I'm disorientated. Used to my lugubrious father and Gavin's masturbatory ramblings, I can't believe how much ground we cover. She talks of her life in Albania; a husband who drank and disappeared, a fifteen-year-old daughter left behind to finish school. But the story is hard to follow, with confusing gaps and time unaccounted. My life sounds dull, each year the same as the last. As she expresses concern for the shivering elephants and emaciated whale, I watch her teeth and lips, amazed there's so much to say. Her wrist is delicate as the stem of her wine glass, my hand beside hers blunt as a flipper. How hard it is to tell the truth, to open drawers and show the broken things inside. A cold sweat slides beneath my shirt while I tear a beer mat into mushy pieces.

She reaches up and touches my face.

I push back my chair, mutter something and leave the pub. Then I'm running. I can jog further and faster these days; my thighs don't chafe and breasts no longer wobble. There's a rock in my throat. The streetlights swim in my eyes and I'm twelve — the night Dad and I went out to look for my mother, searching the streets, calling.

My father crying.

Police cars outside in the dark.

I barely remember my childhood after that. The house filled up with silence and useless shoplifted goods. I was hungry all the time with a drilling want. The padding around me got thicker and thicker. And a zip opened up in me that would never pull closed.

My father didn't expect me home so soon. He looks up from the TV in alarm.

"What's up, son?"

"What happened to Mum? How did she do it? No one ever told me."

I'd never been ready to hear.

"She walked in front of a lorry on the bypass. She was wearing her best dress."

He sighs as if dropping something. Because we're quiet men, there's nothing else to say.

Next day I return home late from *Blue Lizard*. My father is leafing through a recipe book — today's pointless booty, no doubt. He seems unusually animated.

"Your friend Irena's here. She brought your coat back," he says.

I scan our tiny kitchen. "Where?"

"Upstairs. I sent her to bed," he says.

"What?"

"She's shattered. She could hardly keep awake."

As I head, perplexed, for the stairs he calls, "She's really nice, son!"

Irena lies on my bed asleep. Dusk has entered the room ahead of me, smudging the edges of things. I make out her shape on top of the covers and when I lean over, the blurred details of her face. She looks younger than when awake. I feel myself slide and am lonely: for her, for myself. I lie down carefully on the bed beside her. Inching closer, I gently arrange her arm around my neck. Then I sleep.

Even before I wake I know she's gone. The duvet next to me is cool and pulled smooth. It's three in the morning, the hour when everything hurts. She must have been repelled, frightened, to wake beside my bulk. Remembering Gavin's jibes about sows so heavy they must be separated from their piglets in case they crush them, I need to get out of the house and run.

Descending the stairs in my baggy tracksuit, I hear my dad moving around in the kitchen. Then, the first time in our house for thirty years, a woman's laugh, and his murmuring reply. I open the door to find a party in progress. Irena and my father sit at the table with a pot of tea. Packets of biscuits, probably years beyond their sell-by dates, and unlikely liqueurs surround them. My dad is smiling with crumbs all over his face. You'd think he was drinking tea with an angel.

Irena has opened the cookery book at the index.

"Your dad and me are going on your diet too," she says. "We're looking forward to G. Listen to this: Greek salad, guacamole, guinea fowl."

"Gnocchi, guavas," intones my father. "What the hell are they?"

"I've finished with G. I'm up to W now," I say. "But if you stick around, it'll come by again."

Irena pushes the bottle of Kahlua towards me. Without even considering the alphabet, I pour a drink and celebrate.

DADDY'S GIRL

As the young man rides the escalator into the
underground his face is calm. Tension shows in his hands.
The posters trouble him. Near naked images slip by,
generating emotions that pound like his heart. Thoughts of
his wife intrude, and merge with their stark beauty. Body
knotted, face turned away, Abida's rejection magnifies all
that is ugly within him. A warm wind from the approaching
train stirs his clothes. The door slides open to reveal a
packed carriage. For months he has practiced calm,
learned to make a breath last. Hesitating in the doorway,
he looks around for an empty seat.

A girl near the door sees an exhausted man with a heavy
rucksack. Noticing his trembling hands, she jumps up to
offer her seat. Her skittering mind won't let her sit still.
Nine stations down the line a boy is waiting. He sent a text
this morning. Catching sight of her reflection in the dark
window she feels changed, beautiful. Seventeen years old,
she has no words for her crazy hope. Pop songs circle in
her head, their hackneyed lines fresh with promise.

The man with the rucksack nods his thanks. His eyes
stray involuntarily to her legs, slim and strong in short
skirt. He wonders if his small daughter will grow up like
this. Resting his head against the bag he thinks, Hana. As
if down a tunnel, he glimpses white light as the rucksack
turns red hot, splits and gapes open. The roar that comes

is greater than any words, consumes them before they're spoken.

The girl, counting stations, feels heat on her legs. It makes no sense. A line from a song passes through her head –

Pigeons on ledges outside the station feel the first tremor. When the blast comes they've already risen in the air as if at gunshot. Cracks creep along tunnel walls, fracturing the pipes that run beside. Dogs for miles around whine and tremble at the shudders that follow. The barking continues all afternoon.

A small boy watching TV sees a news flash between cartoons. Less than an hour since the explosion, ambulances and fire engines fill the screen. He tugs the dangling hand of his pregnant mother asleep on the sofa. Arranging toy vehicles on the carpet, he announces, as she wakes bewildered, that he wants to be a fireman when he grows up.

A woman whose oldest son died five years ago in a motorbike accident sees the news flash too. Remembering her other boy went to work on the tube this morning, she jabs out his number with trembling hands. By the time he answers she can scarcely breathe. Scalded with grief, raw like it happened yesterday, she relives her first son's death over and over.

A mentally ill man who hasn't left his house for weeks watches the news and knows, beyond any flicker of doubt, that he's responsible. For months signs have appeared on TV. Something he tried to contain has leached out and contaminated the world he has avoided so long. He hears talking. First whispers, then torrents of blame that drown thought. He shuts windows, draws curtains and waits in the dark for them to come for him.

In a park in a midlands city a slight woman, shrouded in religious dress, pushes her daughter on a swing. She knows nothing of the explosion an hour ago. Abida's English is poor and she rarely watches TV. She is thinking of her husband. Her antipathy is now so intense, so close to revulsion, she can hardly bear to be in the same room. Her diaphragm tightens as she pictures him in another woman's arms. She imagines a girl with bare midriff and exposed bra straps. Perhaps one of the young mothers who gather in the park to smoke and chat, ignoring their children. Images that change with the rhythm of the swing slip tapered fingers into her brain. She lets them come, feeds from them, determined to expel him from her heart once and for all.

He didn't come home last night. For months he's been distant and silent, turning to her only for food, or hasty, agitated sex that leaves her hollow and wide eyed in the dark. He speaks just to criticise and belittle. He says she lets too much of her body show, yet she suspects there's another he prefers. To placate him she has toned down her clothes, abandoning her pretty salwar kameez for dark coverings that expose only face and hands. Meanwhile she shops for exquisite outfits for her daughter. Searching chain stores and Indian shops, she finds comfort in pink or turquoise dresses adorned with embroidery and mirrors.

63

She dreams of shoes bejewelled with sequins, so dainty only a child might wear them.

All week her husband has come and gone on unexplained errands, his face tight as a fist. Unable to settle, he picked at her, denounced her hair-dryer and cut labels off her clothes as decadent. She kept out of his way while his disapproval eddied around their tiny house, stifling her.

I'm leaving, I'm leaving, thinks Abida, as the swing goes back and forth.

Yet her imagination fails. She knows little of this country beyond the terrace house she spends hours cleaning, the park and the short walk to Hana's school. Outside flickers a strange, hostile world glimpsed on unintelligible TV and in the doomy warnings of old men at the mosque. Her childhood home and mother seem equally remote. For a moment she lets herself walk through the dusty yard to her mother's house, mind uncluttered, loving nobody.

The child on the swing feels happiness surge as she tenses and relaxes her body with every push. The chains are cool and sturdy against her hot palms. Her new, sequinned, sandals flash in the sunlight. On each upswing Hana's heart soars, then plummets as gravity drags her back. The sky is faded blue like Amy's eyes. For weeks the two children have watched and circled each other warily, both exiled by shyness from the primary coloured effervescence of reception class. Yesterday their gradually diminishing orbit ceased and they collided as if by accident in the playground.

Amy said, "I like your shoes."

Hana politely admired the other girl's navy sandals. Soon they were comparing clothes and hair. Hana liked the look of their hands side by side, though Amy's marbled veins disturbed her.

"Why do your glasses make your eyes look so big?" she asked. It had troubled her for weeks.

"I was born with cataracts," Amy said, with well rehearsed dignity. "I had an operation to take them out when I was a baby, but I've got to wear these glasses until I grow up. I can't see very well really."

Hana, not knowing what to say, didn't reply. Clasping hands they wandered round the playground. From time to time they exchanged details of likes and dislikes: colours, TV programmes, animals — a primitive, delicate offering of selves.

"My favourite animal is ferrets!" said Amy. "We've got two in the garage, in a hutch."

Her descriptions of wiffly noses and see-through ears entranced Hana, who'd never heard of them.

"If you hold them under their front legs, gently so you don't hurt them, they go long and stringy like snakes," Amy said. "You have to keep your face away because they bite. But I won't let them hurt you."

"They sound lovely!" said Hana.

"I've got two pairs of fairy wings at home. Can you come and play at my house?" Amy asked.

Hana spoke to her father about this yesterday evening. She found him in the kitchen staring at his hands, yet irritable and preoccupied as if she interrupted something important. She sidled up and leant against him, keeping her face away from the large beard he'd recently grown.

"Baba, do you like my shoes?"

He grunted, not looking.

"Baba, will you buy me some glasses?"

He noticed her then. "Don't be silly. There's nothing wrong with your eyes."

"Can I play at Amy's house?"

"Who?"

"My friend from school. She wears glasses and she's got ferrets."

"Dirty animals."

Hana was shocked. For the first time she wondered if her father didn't know everything. Maybe he hadn't heard of ferrets or worse, was afraid of their teeth.

"They're clean! Amy says they smell lovely. She won't let them bite me."

Her father said, "We don't know these people."

Shortly afterwards he left the house.

"Amy, Amy," Hana sings as she swings.

The sky has windows and through them she sees visions of games and secrets, fantastic gardens of friendship. Wearing glasses and fairy wings, the two children dance with deliciously elongated ferrets. Never has a child loved her friend so much. Like the girl on the train, Hana is filled with hope.

Tomorrow a small boy will change his mind. His mother will give birth and he'll not want to be a fireman, but a baby again.

A grieving mother will cry all day for her son.

A psychotic man will tremble waiting behind closed curtains.

A little girl won't go to school. Police cars and TV crews will come in the night. Her friend's fear of her will be the first crack. Aftershocks from the explosion will injure all the days of her life.

But now, Hana is happy. As the swing reaches its highest point she doesn't want to come down. For a moment she flies with fairy wings. She is brave like Baba. She is Daddy's girl.

NEEDLE-STICK BABY

My hands are red to the wrist. Blind and clumsy in outsized rubber gloves, my fingers probe the uterus to find the incision again. The nurse scoops blood from the opened abdomen into a metal bowl. She pours it through a sieve and back into the patient via a hanging drip bag and tube. Fast as she bales the level rises. I locate the cut and through it, a small hard head. My fingers inch along slippery curves of back and buttock, hook miniature armpits, slide the baby through the opening and into Angela's hands. She wraps the little boy deftly and continues ladling.

Trembling with tension, I detach the placenta from its gritty bed and drop it into a bucket. The barely anaesthetised mother murmurs. Frustrated by blunt instruments and limited skills, I feel a quick jolt of anger. With looping stitches I secure the gaping uterus. Angela still ladles but the lake is subsiding. The patient is stirring as I close the abdominal wall. No bikini-line incision this, just straight up and down — the fastest way to get the baby out. The needle slides too easily through wasted muscle and paper-fine skin.

Nothing is as it should be. Pregnant women are supposed to be fat. I never claimed to be a surgeon or an obstetrician, but there's only me left. Without a word — no mention of Hippocrates or duty — doctors slid one by one into the night, taking x-ray plates, sterilizer and any equipment that could be sold. Nurses followed with bed linen and bandages. We operate in the few hours when the generator works, by the light of a desk lamp that an auxiliary shines into the wound.

I glance across at the baby tucked beneath the nurse's arm. Calm grey eyes stare back.

I think, Daisy.

The needle snags, slips through thick rubber and pierces my thumb.

There's blood on the floor and inside my plastic boots. At the sink I strip off the gloves and hold my hand beneath guttering brown water. The puncture wound is beginning to ooze, the skin around bruising fast. I look again at the teenage mother. Skin pitted, eyes in dark craters, she's clearly unwell. She mumbles as the anaesthetic, delivered through a soaked rag on her face, wears off.

I've been too long at the sink. Angela looks over my shoulder.

"Are you alright, David?"

Seeing the needle-stick injury, her eyes meet mine in the glass. Later she comes to my on-call room. We lie together, as often before, on the narrow bed. I've no idea what she means to me, or I to her. We never question each other's past or discuss the future.

I rarely leave the hospital now. The streets are dangerous; snipers take pot-shots at cars and pedestrians. And I can't face my flat. Though she left two years ago, some of my wife's clothes still hang in the wardrobe and makeup litters the dressing table. Every hastily half emptied drawer releases potent fumes of rejection. At night, or in moments between patients, I fantasise scenes of her return. She says it was a mistake. Or she just went to find Daisy. Sometimes I imagine she brings our daughter home. Daisy's absence is like a glass splinter in the foot. By treading carefully I avoid feeling it, but when I forget and put down my heel, the pain, after two years, is the same.

My wife never forgave me for sending away our beautiful ten-year-old girl. But there was no choice. All the children were evacuated.

"Why can't you accept it? Daisy is different," she said.

Surely I was right. The city went bad so fast, with burnt-out cars piled into roadblocks and bullet holes in every wall. The kids that remain, darting between shadows and doorways, are feral. I remember Daisy waving excitedly from the coach window as if on a school trip. Instead she was taken to the coast and a ship bound for an unnamed safe destination. All the women were crying. We were promised newsletters and regular e-mails home. We have heard nothing.

Sometimes I lose the will to get up and work. I lie in my clothes from the previous day, weighed down as if with extraordinary gravity, and ignore the uproar outside. Nobody queues quietly anymore; such courtesies now seem quaint and improbable. Patients bang on the clinic door, tear it open and crowd around me. The strong fight the weak to push themselves or their relatives forward. Having so little to give I'm afraid of their disappointment and anger. Mostly I tell them what to buy from the street peddlers who sell pillaged drugs outside the hospital gate. Antibiotics and analgesics are sold like talismans, one pill at a time. I've bartered the dwindling contents of my flat for surgical gloves. People mill around, giddily panic-buying, until a bullet bouncing off the pavement or an explosion a few streets away makes them retreat inside.

Inert on the bed I imagine my wife's return. She says she's sorry, she knows now she can't love anyone but me. I tell myself this story so often, embellished with little details of tenderness and contrition, that for moments at a time I believe it's true. Intrusive, more plausible images of her with that man, I reject. I pretend I don't know who he is.

Sometimes I hear my wife say, "I've found Daisy, she's fine. She was looked after all the time."

I picture Daisy on a beach. The image comes unbidden, awake or asleep. Fallen trees lie twisted into giant lattices on the shore. Waves rear and collapse in great slabs of sound. She's sunburnt, crusted with salt but not unhappy as she plays with shells or climbs the trellis of trees. At night she lies quietly on the sand. She shivers, but doesn't wake.

Daisy has Down's syndrome. In my dream she's not alone. Someone watches over her.

Then Angela comes to fetch me. She pushes my feet into shoes, splashes my face with water and I return to work.

Don't presume I'm a brave man. When they came with guns to rob the pharmacy, I handed over the keys and stood aside without a word. Night after night they return. Sometimes they take women from the wards. I stay in my room and pretend not to hear the sobs and pleading as girls are led away. Equipment and drugs still arrive sporadically in trucks with names of aid agencies on the side. Tough, edgy drivers negotiate roadblocks and landmines to deliver supplies that are stolen within days.

The crowds in the waiting room terrify me. My throat fills with heartbeats so I can scarcely breathe. Each tight layer of fear that I manage to peel away reveals another beneath. Then Angela takes over. I hear her crisp voice outside the clinic door insist on a queue. Passing down the line, she picks out the sickest children to ensure they're seen first. She assumes good will and cooperation, and it works — a sleight of hand that amazes me though I've seen her perform it a hundred times.

Meanwhile I wait. Piece by piece I relinquish all I have. When there's nothing left I'll go. For two years I've waited for my wife to come back. I feel her presence as though she's watching me. If I turn my head to a black splash of shadow, I'm certain she's there. I imagine her admiration — never expressed when we were together — as I operate or cope with impossible cases. A commentary incessant as tinnitus runs through my head while I work.

"Look what I'm doing. I'm better than him. Aren't I?"

It's a relief of sorts, my illness four months after the needle-stick injury. The anticipation and dread are over. My skin flushes hot and cold. Tender mounds form in the hollows of my body and my tongue is coated with white dust. We long ago ran out of kits, but the test is unnecessary. Points of darkness dance before my eyes. Angela's skin feels cool against mine yet I don't pull her closer. There's no need for either of us to say anything.

After ten days the fever subsides. I wake one evening to lightness, as if something has fallen away. Outside, the silence is stretched tight. At last I have nothing. I can go find the beach and my daughter. I'll step through the hospital gate into the filth of the city. I'm prepared to walk through sniper fire, continents, and all the broken doorways of the world. My rucksack is light, so meagre are my needs.

Raindrops explode in puddles as I cross the empty car park. The hospital is in darkness; light shines only from the children's ward. As if space walking, I drift towards it. I step inside to find Angela with the needle-stick baby. His young mother left one night, slipped back into the whispering alleys from where she came. Like all our orphaned and abandoned children, the little boy sleeps in a plastic tub warmed underneath by hot water in a metal bowl. Angela's face is grey and tired, but she smiles as she dips over the cot. The baby waves star-man hands and grins gummily back.

I say, "I'm leaving."

Angela doesn't reply. They are playing peek-a-boo, as if untouched by the days that surround them. She hides behind her hands. Each time her face magically reappears, the baby laughs.

I wonder whether I've spoken aloud.

I say, "Why do you stay?"

Angela glances up. "I'm needed here."

She covers her face again. "And for you, David."

Like a pianist who has practised the same bars over and over, I hear for the first time the tune that was there all along.

She says, "A girl on the post-natal ward is bleeding. I've got the theatre ready. I'm glad you're feeling better. I didn't want to wake you."

I put my bag down. Angela fishes the wriggling baby from his plastic bowl and hands him to me. Compared with my rucksack the child is substantial, chunky. Grabbing my finger ferociously, he stares as if I'm the shiniest thing he's ever seen.

Running on the Right Side of the Brain

Taut in fluorescent Lycra, the runners radiate belligerent vitality. As she watches them limber up, Eve's fantasies of lolloping over the hills in a friendly pack fade. The mountain, indifferent to squats and stretches, looms behind them.

"Get your handbag off, chook," a spectator yells. It sounds indecent. "You can't go shopping up there. And you can't run in sunglasses!"

Seized by panic she wonders, why not?

A starting pistol cracks. The competitors shoot across a field and up the mountain, her friend Clare, instigator of this folly, in close pursuit. Eve stumbles after, reviewing her humble ambitions. First, to complete the race and second, an absurd conceit, to finish anywhere but last.

Jogging along at the rear Eve watches the contestants disappear into the distance, their colourful bodies soon hidden behind outcrops of rock. Presently she realises she's not the only laggard. Others are running at her measured pace: a damp, obese man; a sullen teenage girl; a vague woman, Eve's doppelganger, with handbag and sunglasses. She realises smugly she can overtake all three. No one responds to her jaunty greetings as she passes — perhaps they can't breathe. Her chest thumps in alarm but she reaches the top surprisingly soon. The mountain deceived her. The race is much shorter than she thought.

"Don't think you can run in front of me. You have to go round!"

A surly steward leans against a cairn bearing a flag. He evidently believes she can improve, by cheating, her woeful position in the event. She's flattered he thinks the effort worth it.

Going down is harder. Eve's cheap trainers have no grip and she can't keep her feet. As she tumbles over tussocks and skids on shale, fat man, sulky girl and handbag woman overtake her in quick succession. They hail her, but Eve ignores them. She's last again, her ephemeral triumph a mockery. Everyone has disappeared. Overtaken by an easy rhythm she runs on, enjoying the sensation of feet on grass. Somewhere else, time passes. Mountains stretch to both sides. She watches the light on them harden as the sun shrinks to a cold knot. Eve shivers as her sweat dries. She hasn't seen flag or steward for ages. No one at all. Two elderly dog walkers amble towards her.

"Is there a race on?" they ask. "We've not seen anyone else, duck."

The cardboard number flaps against her chest, clownish and unlucky as a toupee. She strips it off. The men proffer a map, which she turns upside-down hoping for enlightenment. Paths and contours rotate unhelpfully. By veering right not left several times, she is lost.

She remembers numerous journeys with the same outcome. While she daydreams, her body makes random choices at crossroads. She misses turn-offs, goes back and overshoots again; or searches mazes of streets for a clue — memorable tree or garden gnome — to the exit. In this way she has squandered her life.

Eve recalls a wine fuelled conversation with Clare.

She had claimed — an inauspicious boast — to drive with her brain in neutral. She described instants when, sliding between two states of consciousness, she freezes at traffic lights unable to recollect why red turns green. For split seconds she forgets the function of the control pedals.

Clare said, "If you can drive with your brain in neutral, why not put it in reverse?"

Lost on a mountain, tired of herself, Eve decides impulsively to do so. She will put her brain into reverse. Re-do everything. Delete the mistakes.

It's easier than she thought. She feels something contract as the meninges pull away from her skull. No pain, merely a pleasant sucking like a child's love bite, followed by a sudden, bucking, gravitational force. Muscles begin to work backward, contractions rippling up instead of down like salmon swimming upstream. Legs and arms in unfamiliar motion pump back to front. Scenery trembles out of focus as her eyes adjust. Disorientated, seized by vertigo, she runs backwards up hill. Back past obese man, morose girl and handbag woman. Confused, until she realises they were behind her in time, not space. Her fatigue recedes. Stronger by the minute she retraces her steps up the mountain, widdershins.

As she runs she gathers up the wasted time. Years spent looking for things: purses, keys, success, love. Before they break, she catches glasses and plates dropped from her clumsy or nervous fingers. She watches the beer tipped on a stranger in a bar, flow upward. As the stain retreats, his frown ebbs into the social smile before the blunder.

Now she has the hang of it. She deletes them all. The gaffes, pratfalls and catastrophic mistakes. Crass words; inappropriate eye contact; affection declared to someone baffled, not reciprocating: gone. A bosom flopping from a bikini top is hauled back in — it never happened. Her car, backed into a lamppost, unbuckles. The metal untwists with a thunderous sound, passing from silence back to silence. Contraceptives that pop, or drop out and shoot across the room, are retrieved. Here Eve hesitates and decides not to intervene, because where would be the children? At last her momentum fails. Trainers dragging on shale, she slows to a momentary halt.

Then as if propelled from a catapult, she shoots forward again. Lighter, blander, all her mistakes removed, she has time to observe the bungles and dithering of others. How restful to watch, detached as God, while others prang cars. Or pull on doors marked 'Push' and fracture their skulls. Planes drop from the sky: air traffic control has mistaken left for right again! Surgeons energetically amputate the wrong limb — so easily done. A president's finger wavers indecisively between two buttons, one marked, 'Armageddon,' the other, 'Better not!' How simple, Eve thinks, to muddle them up.

She passes her father, long dead, reading in an armchair by the side of the path. His legs are crossed and he wriggles his toes, the same as hers, a familiar pose. She catches a beer mug as it falls from his hand. Remembering that she forgot before, or had no time, she tells him she loves him.

"I know," he shouts after her as she runs on. "I always knew."

In the distance she sees the place where the race began. The finishing line is stretched between two posts. Miniature people mill around or move towards their cars. Shadows from the mountain lie down in folds for the night. The fell race is over.

Clare is waiting fretfully, lithe in Lycra as an eel in a condom.

"Where have you been?" she shouts as Eve runs towards her. "I finished ages ago. They sent the winner back to find you. You're hours behind!"

Eve although dishevelled is hardly breathless. She crosses the finish line to subdued jeers and kindly patronage from the few remaining spectators.

"You know," Clare says, watching Eve dust herself down, "I think the run has done you good. You look ten years younger."

The Crow Down the Chimney

You said, "Let's just walk until we reach the border and then we'll nearly be home."

In the darkness by the railway track you seemed the same as before. Most kids changed after they were sent away.

"What border?" I asked.

"There's always a border. You cross it and then you're safe."

I imagined a line on the ground somewhere. I'd step over it into our kitchen and see Dad by the fire in his string vest. He'd look up in surprise and say, "Frank! You came home!"

We took turns to kneel with our ears against the rail. Although you're a girl, you knew what to do because your father worked for the railways.

You said, "Once my dad found a hand beside the track. The men missed it when they cleared up the body. I heard him tell Uncle John. He wrapped it in newspaper and took it to the police."

I pictured dead hands moving in the night. They might creep out from behind anything: trees, hedges, buildings.

You said, "Which way is home?"

I'd planned to walk back to Dagenham along the track so I wouldn't get lost. But now the hand squirmed on the ground in the shadows, wrapped in newspaper and struggling to get out. We'd have to go another way.

"We must be careful," you said. "Last time I ran away the police caught me at the station and took me back to the man. They said I was naughty to worry everyone, and lucky to live with him because he's important and has a big house."

"Bailsey thinks I took her purse," I said. "She's got so much stuff. She leaves it lying all over the place. She's always losing things."

"I hate the man," you said. "He looks at me funny. And he keeps kissing me, but not like Daddy or Uncle John. When we get home I'm going to tell my mum."

I didn't know what to say about kisses, Elsie.

The day we left Dagenham Mum said, "It's not for long. The war will be over soon. Then your dad will come home and so can you."

She was crying as she pushed us onto the train. All the kids were sad at first. Then they cheered up and started eating sandwiches. Mine were jam, with cold sweet tea in a bottle. As we left London and passed fields with cows and tractors, everyone began shouting and throwing things about. After a while the rocking train made us sleepy and we went quiet again. At the station in the country people were gathered on the platform. Our teacher had a clip-board, but the grown-ups were picking us out one by one. The girls were chosen first. Then the bigger, stronger boys, by tough men who looked like farmers. My brother Alf soon went. He turned and stared at me as he was led away, clutching his cardboard suitcase. With my thick glasses I knew I'd be one of the last. Mrs Bails who took me was angry.

"Why should I be lumbered with you, just because I've got a spare room?" she said.

Every evening Bailsey dragged a nit comb hard through my hair. She made me hold out my hands to check for scabies. After I used the toilet in the outhouse she threw bleach down it. But we're very particular in our family. Mum says children need a good wash and airing once a week. She disapproves of women whose kids wear the same underwear all winter. At home there's a proper bath with hot water from the copper, not a tin tub in the kitchen like Mrs Bails'. Alf used to share the bath with me on a Sunday, but in his crowd of big boys at school here he seemed different, as if he didn't want to know me. I wanted to talk to him about home sometimes, but felt shy and babyish, so just hung around and then went back to my friends.

In Mrs Bails' house, rats ran around in the roof. At night I'd hear them and think about yellow teeth, greasy fur and worm tails just above my head. Then I'd worry about Dad getting killed by Germans and Mum by a bomb. Bailsey said council houses are dirty, but we don't have a single mouse. My cat Blackie is a brilliant mouser. One night before we came away we were down in the air raid shelter in the garden. Blackie was purring on my lap. Mum kept jumping up, moving things and sitting down again.

She said, "Why doesn't the bloody thing just drop!"

At last she noticed Blackie and laughed so much I thought she was going to choke. Then she grabbed me and Alf to hug us. She'd taken the purring for a doodle-bug. They drone on and on and when it goes quiet, the bomb is about to fall. You hear the explosion and know you're safe because someone else has copped it.

When Bailsey accused me of thieving I was scared. I knew the police would believe her, not me. I'm thin enough

81

to squeeze through anything and my brother says I climb like a monkey. Slipping out the window and down the drainpipe was so easy I wish I'd thought of it before.

I was lucky to find you, Elsie. I didn't like walking in the night. The huge birds lined up on the trees frightened me. They'd take off and fly around screeching, making my heart beat fast. In Dagenham the sky is never black, only grey, and birds are little hopping sparrows, not sharp-beaked monsters. At first I thought people were watching us, but when my eyes got used to the dark it was only sheep. If an animal coughed we both jumped. We walked a long way until our legs were tired. Usually I don't hold hands with girls, but didn't mind you taking mine, your fingers small and cold. At last we come to a farm. The out-buildings were locked and looked empty. Squeezing through a window, we fell onto deep straw and scattered a pile of potatoes.

Inside the barn you were just a ghost against the window, your eyes black holes. The darkness was all over us like cobwebs.

"A crow fell down the chimney," you whispered. "It was alive, but the man threw it back on the fire." I'd never heard anyone's teeth chatter before.

I budged up close and told you a story about the day my dad chucked his boots into the bin. Then Mum cut up his uniform for dusters so he couldn't ever go back to the army. As I spoke I could see them, so real I almost believed it was true.

I said, "But he kept his gun. So if the Germans come, we can see them off."

You stopped trembling. "My dad wasn't called up because he's on the railways. But Uncle John is in the

RAF. If he cuts up his uniform, will they let him come home?"

Sometimes I get muddled about whether things are real or if I've just thought them. But I told you it was true.

When I woke it was light and I was alone. Straight away I thought of dead hands moving the potatoes around. I was hungry, itching and needed the toilet, but too scared to go anywhere without my glasses. There was a smell of breakfast frying from the farmhouse. It was ages since I tasted bacon because Mum could never get any, but maybe farmers eat their pigs. I heard scuffling as you crawled back through the barn window carrying an old metal bowl filled with blackberries and little apples. You spotted my glasses sticking out of the straw and handed them to me.

You said, "There's water in a barrel outside. And apples and blackberries enough for ages."

After breakfast I felt queasy, my stomach hollow. Alf and me used to moan every year when Mum sent us to collect blackberries. Remembering crumble and custard made me sad and hungry, but excited to be going home.

Now we could see a tractor in the barn. I'd never been near such a huge, dangerous machine. I couldn't help it, I had to climb on. Even pulling with all my strength, I couldn't turn the steering wheel an inch.

I said, "If we make it go we'll be home in no time."

You seemed scared again and said, "Come down quickly, Frank. We've got to get out before the farmer comes. He'll be cross about us messing with his tractor."

Outside in the morning sun you looked smaller and younger. The shadows beneath your eyes were blue as a bird's egg. We stood by the road looking both ways and you held my hand again. I didn't know what to do.

You started to cry. "I don't like men, only Daddy and Uncle John and you."

I hugged you like Dad does me when I'm upset. You felt little and bony, but went all loose and leaned against me.

I said, "Don't cry, Elsie. Look, we're nearly at the border."

I pointed across the fields. Where the earth met the sky was a line, I swear. I picked a flower from the hedgerow and twisted it into your hair.

You stopped sniffing and smiled. "Yes, I think I can see it too."

I found you the second time on the platform at Dagenham station. I'd been back to visit my parents. Most people are different after twenty years, but as you stepped into the carriage in that heavy coat, I knew you. At ten I was maybe an inch taller than you, but I doubled in size during the next few years, whereas you seem scarcely to have grown. I moved down the carriage and sat opposite you.

"Elsie?"

You stared and then smiled. "Frank! Well!"

"Well!"

After a short silence you said, "We didn't get far, did we?"

As the train rattled towards Liverpool Street, red brick council houses gave way to allotments like shanty towns of planks and wire. Then mile after mile of terraces with their backs turned to the railway and yards cluttered with washing. Passing Stratford, I told you about my job as reporter for a London paper. By Mile End, you knew of my wife and three-year-old twins. You listened with strained caution, nodding from time to time, until I wondered if I was talking too much.

I said, "What about you? Are you married?"

You shook your head and gazed through the window at a gritty sky. There were still bombed-out gaps between the houses, filled with rosebay willow herb and old sofas.

At Bethnal Green you said, "I don't remember seeing you afterwards, at school or anywhere. I wonder why not."

My memories of that time were like eddying water. There was a tractor and I lost my glasses. Only the caning at school for stealing and running away remained vivid. When my mother heard, she sent for me to come home.

I said, "I didn't stay. My mother said you can harm a child in more ways than bombs. If we were going to die she reckoned we should all go together. The teacher said she was irresponsible, but I was happy. I never believed the bombs would touch us."

"Your mother was right. They sent me back to the same bloke. I spent the rest of the war there."

"Did you run away again?"

"No. He made damn sure of that."

An injured bird tossed onto a fire. With a sudden heart-knock, I realised this recurring image from the shifting borders of sleep was yours.

I said, "What do you do now?"

"I never really worked. By the time the war finished, Mother was ill. My Uncle John's plane was shot down and she never got over it. I stayed home to look after her. After she died I kept house for my father. Last year he went too."

The carriage lights flickered as the train trundled through a tunnel. The greasy darkened window reflected your face, turned away.

After a moment you said, "I haven't been well in myself, Frank. Not for a long time."

"I'm sorry. Nothing serious, I hope."

"My doctor says it's not really his thing, so got me to see a ... specialist he knows. That's why I'm going up to town. I have an appointment every month."

I said, "Does it help?"

"Sort of. I can leave the house now. But he says there's too much I won't tell him."

We were back in the barn. I thought of a dead hand, moving.

I said, "Is there?"

The train pulled into Liverpool Street. Pigeons with broken feet picked crumbs from the platform. The high glass roof arched like a sky they could never reach. You tightened the belt of your coat and stood up, looking small, gaunt and older than you should. The shadows beneath your eyes were still bird's egg blue. I wanted to put my arms round you.

You said, "I'm glad you got away, Frank."

We leaned together.

I said, "Tell me. Tell me about the crow down the chimney."

You touched my arm and we walked towards the ticket barrier and the station cafe. I hesitated and looked back down the track. Where we'd come from, in the distance where the rails met the sky, I swear there was a line.

ONE HUNDRED DAYS

I haven't seen my face in the mirror since I arrived in this country. If I narrow my eyes and concentrate there's a suggestion of cheekbone or jaw sinking back as if into sand. Sometimes I study my passport photo, but don't suppose I look so young now. Glancing sideways into shop windows I see only outline and shadow.

As a young man I'd pause, razor in hand, and smile at my reflection.

My mother said, "Amos, you'll crack that thing."

I learnt early, practiced the downward glance and half smile, the precise amount and quality of attention. By eighteen I'd slept with every girl I wanted in the villages all around. Of course my height was an advantage. But I always knew I'd leave to be a writer or poet in the city, with a woman who didn't smell of wood smoke.

When I look in the mirror I see other faces: my wife's or my children's; more often, the mayor's. Or through curled smoke and flickering shadows, mouths stretched and screaming, the faces of girls I knew. Thatched huts burning like hair. My body changes temperature and I turn away.

I have lost my wife and kids. They fled into the bush on the first day. Returning from work I found the ransacked hut empty but for my books, scattered like injured birds, and the mirror broken on the floor. Gone: my baby boy, Solomon. My big girl, Margaret. I remember the wriggling, hard-packed weight of my little boy, and my daughter arranging stones in patterns by the fire while my wife stirred the cooking pot. Margaret would be old enough to marry now.

When I think of my wife I remember only detail. The curve of cheek and breast; fingers curled around a bowl. She changed so quickly from the woman I wanted her to be. She worried constantly about money and the bad rains and the children getting ill. After our third child was stillborn she didn't stop bleeding. She moved to her sister's house and sat all day by the washed-out cloths she wore for the blood, so that no one could steal them from the line to harm us with magic. All I could see was an anxious, superstitious woman, crouched in the dirt beside her stained rags. My love for her hardened and shrank to a kernel.

After one hundred days, silence fell and soaked the earth. The usual morning sounds — dogs barking, women calling to each other as they tended the fires for the breakfast cooking pots, cocks crowing — were absent. I gathered my belongings and left, carrying with me the smell that hung thick over the village. Others were walking, heads lowered or swinging from side to side like baited animals. Some had injuries I cannot describe. I passed villages, flattened and flayed. Doors swung open on desecrated schools and churches. People lay by the side of the road; my mind registered, but tried to substitute more recognisable rubble. Vacant-eyed children squatted in the scant shade of telegraph poles. I walked through days and nights like broken glass. Mostly my head was empty as the sky. Or else I argued with someone, maybe my wife, changing words and sentences to make myself clear. Although she hadn't looked me in the face for a long time, in my imagination I continued to reason with the woman I wanted her to be. At every border I grew through another self. I crossed three countries and every language was stranger than the last, until I understood nothing. Then I came to the town where my cousin lived.

An air ticket, a passport and a tale to tell. A story I nearly believed, like those I spun for the village girls a lifetime ago.

I gave it up. The red earth and hot, fickle rain, the sun that rises fast pulling colour behind it like a train, exchanged for a visa and a job stacking boxes in a distant grey city. I left the work I'd had since school, in the mayor's office where I added figures and registered births and deaths. I'd wanted so much more. I was my mother's first born, her darling. Our meagre village lacked book or radio. The only escape was secondary school, so my mother worked on a coffee plantation to pay for my education. Her stories of my father were vague, but I guessed. Even as a child I was a head taller than the rest; soon I was two, then three. In my teens, transfixed by the mirror, I watched myself elongate: first limbs, then jaw and nose, until I imagined I looked like him.

"Hey you! Big boy, giraffe man! Hey Amos!"

Village children, naked or adorned in rags more symbolic than functional, cartwheeled behind me yelling.

The lists I kept for the mayor grew longer. Everyone was allocated a tribe, though we lived side by side in the villages and had intermarried for generations. Each identity card I issued confirmed, in my beautiful handwriting, an individual's ethnic group. When people were hazy I guessed. Years passed in a reverie, my head full of poetry as I dreamed of better things. Sunblind, I failed to see what was coming. Perhaps at some level I understood: the half-heard phone calls; the mayor's appraising look; his shrug like a bribe. Through long afternoons I sweated at my desk, in the dark suit my wife pressed every evening with the fire-iron.

The mayor's face, empty as a plate, fills the mirror now.

I stack boxes in a storeroom in a cold English city, beneath harsh artificial light that throws no shadows. Lorries arrive by day and night and I record deliveries in a book. My back bends and arms move with their own rhythm. I feel my body soften, muscles waste, as I expend my strength on air. Only the blood in my head is hot and loud. I've built a fence of mirrors around the past. I guard it vigilantly and it works, reflecting back only the moment. For hours at a time I don't think. Instead I count, or lose myself in small sensations. I barely speak this language. Words squirm just out of reach. My voice, strange and thick as if from a mouthful of mud, echoes in this Spartan place of white walls and brown cardboard.

The machetes started to arrive in lorry loads. My job was to count them in, number them and write it down in ledgers. The trucks came first at night and then by day, delivering implements that I lined up in the mayor's warehouse. They brought other tools: knives, mallets, scythes — sharp or heavy things for slashing and crushing.

The voices on the radio changed. They spoke of the thin soil and insufficient rain. The poor health of our children. Yet some people, the tall ones, had more than the rest.

Their children have shoes. Their wives are fat from sucking dry the teat of this country. Why are they so tall?

Because they've always had too much of everything. See in
your own village. Like cockroaches, they eat what they find.
We've waited too long. We must get ready.

Words insidious like damp that finds a way in.

Meanwhile the heat grew. The sky stayed blank as God,
the sun his hot eye. The time for rain came and went
without a cloud, just as it had for three years. All the
children had orange patches in their hair. Some had water
beneath the skin, stretching their feet and bellies.

The radio said, *The time has come. Let it begin.*

The mayor eyed me up and down, a curious flatness in
his voice.

"Amos, the size of you — you'd better stay sitting if you
want to keep your looks."

People queued at the door. Women with babies on their
backs, grandparents, children. Silence, excitement. Nobody
looked at anyone else. No one looked at me as I handed out
the machetes, first by night and then by day. I opened a
new ledger for the next one hundred days.

The mayor said, "If they know what's good for them
they'll gather at the school. Amos, take the bicycle. Seek
them out. Tell them, go to the school and we'll protect
them. If not we can't be responsible for their safety."

Sweating in my suit I bumped along rutted roads to half
emptied villages that waited like a bride too young to
understand. Nothing breathed but stupid chickens
pecking. Many of the women were my teenage girlfriends. It
worked again: the downward glance, my eyes on theirs for
just the right number of seconds, as I checked ledgers and
wrote names in my beautiful handwriting.

Now I live on the other side of the earth. The city is a mesh of shouts and machines, the traffic a steady grey noise. I begin again in a woman's arms. Nasma: she too is exiled, from a country more alien than I can imagine. Her golden skin is tarnished; deep lines bracket her mouth and eyes. She searches the streets for something lost, jumps at the slightest sound — in my village they would call her crazy. We hardly speak. When we make love she passes through doors that swing shut in my face. But in the white hour before dawn we lie side by side holding hands like children who have seen nothing.

Tonight I saw the mayor on the news.

Most evenings, to improve her English, Nasma watches TV. She repeats sentences for me slowly. When she leaves the room I'm afraid I'll disappear. The meaningless images flicker and slip as I divide time in half, split it again and again into diminishing fragments until only the moment remains. All day as I wait for her to come home or my shift to end, I create these instants that contain nothing but the present.

But now I listen.

"*One hundred days –*"

Even in this strange tongue the words seek me out.

There's a photo of the mayor looking smaller than I remember, smiling outside a British house. Another more blurred of him presiding at a wedding back home. I recognise the place, even the trees, and peer at the faces.

Nasma says, "They're talking about your country. They've caught six of them living over here. The organisers."

My body tingles like an amputation. I stand up and lurch to the bathroom. In the mirror the mayor is there again, his eyes devoid of human spark. Then he's gone and I'm looking through the school door at people huddled within. I recognise all the faces but can't hear a sound. The shadows resolve into bodies, felled and felling. Men cut down boys, children hack old people. I see women beaten, their cloths torn away. But they're not just women: they are the girls I knew.

"Amos, what is it?"

Nasma is beside me. She wraps her arms around my trembling shoulders and pulls my head down level with hers. In the mirror she sees what I can't — the two of us staring. Then my face is there, moving towards us in the glass. But I don't want to see. I'm frightened.

I am not that kind of man.

Pump It Up

In the wall to wall mirror Eve watches the man writhe. His cheeks and lips stretch, his eyes protrude. Unable to bear the grunts, she proffers her dumbbells.

"Try mine. They're much lighter."

His face implodes into wrinkles.

"I think I've just popped something," he says.

"Steady on."

He puts down his weights and shakes his arms.

"I'm here five days a week and it's still agony," he confides.

"The mirrors are the worst thing," Eve says. "We all look ridiculous."

He shrugs and takes up his weights. Eve wanders off to find a machine, satisfied with this exchange. Conversation at the gym is rare; everyone so preoccupied with their indelicate rituals that even a smile would intrude. From the wobbly vantage of a step machine she studies people. Men groan on benches as if in the throes of bad sex or constipation. They leave sweat angels on the mats. The women are silent and intent. Some, about Eve's age, are pared down like raddled, twitchy pipe cleaners. Skull-faced girls obsessively record schedules in notebooks. Crones perched on space hoppers lift sponge weights to music.

To prevent complacency, illustrations of the perfect human form are everywhere. As she runs up and down virtual hills, Eve watches three huge T.V. screens. One plays endless pop videos. The bland music is spiced with racy images. Girl dancers posture like baboons, so improbably wanton they appear insane. The next shows a fifties religious movie. As Jesus toils up the hill to be crucified, Eve's eyes flick back and forth between Calvary and baboon women. The third, a boxing match. The commentator drones on while a young man is punched in the face. Eve keeps running.

Bored with weights and machines, she decides to join an exercise class. The instructor, a diminutive woman in baseball cap and string vest, flexes her biceps, which bulge impressively. Cheered that she need no longer aspire to waif-like skinniness, Eve immediately decides she too wants muscles. She imagines herself Pansy Potter the strong man's daughter, lugging compost bags around the garden without compromise to her pelvic floor.

Oddly exhilarated, she waves little dumbbells around. Mirrors on three sides reflect the class to infinity. Corridors of ever-shrinking people lift weights to horrible music. A man at the back moves left as everyone steps right and falls off his box. She watches in the mirror as he does it again and again, finally dropping his weights on the floor. Why is he here? Eve wonders. What does he think he's doing?

She hasn't been to anything like this for years. Once, long ago, she attended an aerobics class. Too proud to prance in striped leotard, she never went back. Now dainty is out. Everyone, male and female, aspires to powerful thighs and muscles of magnitude.

The mixed gender class is disconcerting. Legs akimbo, gussets reflected in the mirrors, they ignore, like the emperor's new clothes, sexual parallels. Beside Eve is the bull-necked man she addressed earlier. She regrets her boldness. He lies with thighs wide apart like a monster on its slab. She averts her eyes, chilled by the thought of his atrophied testicles reflected to infinity. He fixes twenty kilogram weights on his bar while she toys with tiny ones.

"You can pile on more than that, duck," he says.

He ambles away to fetch her more weights. Alarmed by his solicitude, she suspects he favours squat women, just as Sumo wrestlers prefer miniscule girlfriends to accentuate, by contrast, their bulk. The next exercise begins. The class jut out their buttocks like the baboon women and crouch up and down. With steroid man lurking behind her, Eve can't concentrate.

One young man, on his knees, has piled up so many weights he can't stand. Eve is concerned; he appears to be in pain. He should be in bed with his girlfriend on Sunday morning, not busting a gut with middle-aged tossers. He seems determined and conscientious. Surely a girl somewhere will love him for this, rather than the six-pack that eludes him.

No friend of Eve's ever suggested that 'abs' were an essential, even desirable, requirement for a lover. In the gym they abound, in virtual form at least, and are discussed at length. Feeling ill informed, she consults the magazines that lie around. She flicks through 'Men's Health,' expecting articles on prostates and penile complaints. Then spotting a facet of the male psyche usually concealed from women, reads avidly.

'Don't worry if in bed with a new girlfriend, you find she has grey underwear, an untended bikini line or hairy legs.'

Eve reads on marvelling. What do men know of such things?

'Women use these like a chastity belt. A reminder of sexual restraint. If her panties are baggy, congratulate yourself. She's gone to bed with you before she intended.'

Eve reflects uneasily that all her knickers are like that. No wonder her husband is so smug.

'Women always complain there's not enough foreplay. Give them twenty minutes. If necessary set a timer.'

Eve pities the girl in baggy drawers. As her new beau sets the stopwatch she must regret her impetuosity. Nor is she likely to recover her ardour when the timer pings. 'Men's Health,' having titillated its readers so far, omits further advice. Instead follow page after page of misshapen men. At their feet, or over their torsos, lie grinning girls who depilated until they lost their wits. Eve reflects that men and women journey on different sexual railway trains. The tracks run parallel and they wave in a friendly way from the windows but never quite connect. One might expect male and female fantasies to dovetail, but reading 'Men's Health,' she doubts it.

Later she has a fitness assessment. Bored stiff, a young man named Kirk encourages her to mount elaborate scales. She hears bleeps, and a printout covered in figures shoots from a slot. Kirk pretends to study the information intently. Her weight is unchanged.

"Two pounds of your fat have turned to muscle," Kirk announces.

"I doubt it," Eve says. "How can a machine tell that, just by me standing on it?"

"There's an electric current that goes through the skin –" he begins, and then falters. "Actually, I don't know."

She shouldn't have challenged Kirk. She has no wish to nudge him prematurely onto the step machine of self doubt and cynicism that we all must ultimately tread. Not when he's so muscley and everything.

"Perhaps it's just a rough guide," she suggests.

Kirk tries again. "It seems you're better hydrated this month. Have you been drinking more fluids?"

"No."

They regard each other mournfully. Kirk is lost for words.

"I'm really hungry," he says at last. "I've been here since six this morning."

"Why don't you go and have lunch?"

She doesn't want to trouble him. He's only young and if he reads those ludicrous magazines, has enough to worry about.

What's the point? Manoeuvring the wheelie bin down the garden steps doesn't get easier. Nor do her biceps bulge, Popeye-style, through her tee shirt. The gym provides shelter and a useful insight into male vanity. Gloomy thoughts are trounced by mindless music. Nor can she take silly movements, performed in front of wall-to-wall mirrors, too seriously. For someone with a regrettable tendency to disappear up her own arse, this is beneficial.

Eve returns home, in a narcissistic lather, to her husband slumped in front of the snooker.

"How's steroid man?" Tim murmurs.

Fired up with adrenaline and saucy videos, she's disappointed by his nonchalance. She expects jealous rage, if not Othello.

"How's Toad Neck?" her oldest son joins in.

By coincidence he's applying the final brush strokes to a small model of a toad dressed for battle. He has painstakingly painted its skin 'slime green' and 'putrescent yellow.' The nastily named pots are open on the table. Minute maggots, each segment lovingly highlighted, crawl from warty lesions on its torso. Eve is startled by the likeness to her pumped-up paramour.

"Toad man is in fine form," she says. "He has muscles of magnitude."

But lost in nerdy pursuits, no one is listening.

Her youngest boy stands on a chair, grimacing in the mirror like the men at the gym.

"Tree! I am no tree! I am an Ent!" he announces.

As usual she doesn't know what he's talking about. Flexing her biceps sadly she studies the males in her life, all of whom ignore her. Not one of them knows where his 'abs' are located. They are all Softy Walters to her Pansy Potter, but she wouldn't want them any other way, would she?

STALKER

All summer Jack stalks. Ear to wall, eye to crack, he trails his parents quietly. By the back door, between hedge and fence, he has made a hide.

His mother says, "I can't believe it's her. Not that fat cow."

Jack sees his father flinch. He considers which of them he loves best, or hates least. Like standing on a see-saw, one foot each side, he can tip either way. He is ten, and soon they will ask him to choose.

"Don't talk to me about fucking chemistry," his mother says. "Just don't give me that."

At night they pour silence like concrete. Afraid they will die, he lies down outside their bedroom door.

His father says, "After the divorce –"

Sunlight trickles green-yellow through the leaves of Jack's hide. There's a smell of creosote and cat's piss. He squirts glue into an empty crisp bag, holds it over his mouth and sucks out the air, gags as pain punches his temples.

Words thud at the end of a tunnel. *Fat cow. Chemistry. Divorce.*

Elation flares like a firework. He sucks again and his spirits blast upwards. His head and limbs go light and loose and he doesn't care.

He doesn't fucking care.

His parents exchange glances as Jack enters the kitchen. He knows they can't wait for him to leave so they can hurt each other again. His mother fumbles in her bag with trembling fingers.

"Can you nip out for us, love? Get some milk from the shop?"

"OK, I'll get your fucking milk."

His words echo far away. Did he say that or not? Her expression stays the same. His parents are tiny, wingless things that creep round and around, trapped in a jar. She paces, biting her nails. His father leans blank faced against the wall.

Jack gets as far as the gate and lies down. The earth sweats. Everything is leaking away. A passerby with a dog looks at him curiously. His mother stares from the window and her face alters. He hears the door open. She runs towards him down the path.

Don't even blink, Jack thinks.

HAND OF GOD

Gabrielle is up early for prayers at dawn. The pillow still holds the warm scent of her hair. I shift my head carefully and watch her. She potters around humming, surrounded by an aura of scintillating brightness. Sprawled on my bunk I feel the engine thud and waves crack against the hull. The thought of the depth of sea below brings bile to my mouth.

Since the day we set out I've been ill. Migraine flickers constantly like insect wings at the periphery of my vision. Regularly through the day it overwhelms me and I lie on the bunk, head full of pounding heartbeats and flashing lights, moving only to vomit in a bucket. But there are moments when I see, within shimmering halos, images vivid as a mystic's. I understand with startling clarity everything that's happened. Then I'm retching again. No one expects much of me and I'm left alone. Late for every meeting, I slip in at the back. That's why I see what the others can't.

Six weeks: I scarcely believe it. Time has stretched thin so this voyage has lasted a lifetime. I'm here because Gabby invited me. There was no reason to stay behind. Month after month from the window of my hall of residence, I watched cars stream out of the city. Rivers of retreating vehicles loaded with fridges and carpets, but fewer every week that passed. Most people have gone now, just the old, stubborn and sick left behind. I continued to attend lectures until the tutors didn't show, and studied in the library for exams I no longer believed would happen.

Gabrielle said, "Why are you waiting, Ryan? I'm leaving now. Come with me."

She introduced me to John, our leader. Mid-fifties, imposingly tall, with close cropped grey hair and pouched eyes, he made me uneasy from the start. He asked about my strength and health, and Gabby vouched for my convictions. His even smile flattered yet unsettled me. And still I didn't understand our mission.

"Why South America?" I found myself whispering, even when we were alone. "I thought they were Christian already. Where exactly are we going? And how will we spread the word? John makes it sound like margarine."

I'm not sure that I'm religious, but I've no other word for it. All my life I've had rituals, mostly self invented. In my head, or under my breath, I'm often counting. Prayers are a continuous internal litany. Answers come, but in my voice, or the scripture I recite over and over until meaning is lost and my mind spins in a groove like a gyroscope.

But Gabrielle sees beauty in things. When I'm with her so do I, as if the world has opened a crack. The first day of the voyage I saw it, in the mirrors of light that danced in the wash behind us, the clean empty sea and pale dome of sky. Seagulls wheeled and plunged, and Gabrielle's hair blew across her mouth, providing meaning enough for the journey. Gabby sees depths and shades of colour that I can't imagine. When she talks my skin prickles and I realise what's missing in me.

The first days reminded me of my church youth club. Long-haired girls played simple songs on guitars. Earnest boys gave bible readings. I felt impatient, too old for this now. There was even a ping-pong table, though watching the ball ricochet around the room made my stomach heave. Children were everywhere, unaccompanied evacuees, darting amongst the adults. Daisy, a little girl with Down's syndrome, treated me to a gob-stopping kiss on the lips. Gabrielle was happy and looked like an angel. I'd follow her to the end of the earth.

The first time she came to my bunk I said, "Are you sure?"

I didn't want her to regret anything.

"It's a sacrament," she told me.

That's my girl, I thought. That's my Gabby. No qualms and an answer for anything. I'd make that sacrament any time. She'd ambush me in the corridor to drag me into an empty cabin, or pin me against deck rails while dark water thundered below. I wondered if John knew about us. The thought scared me. From my seat at the back I observed him at the lectern.

One night he said, "Come to the front, all who want to give their life to the Lord."

As if my own beliefs counted for nothing, I found myself walking towards him, propelled by an unknown force. When he'd finished I turned, shocked and exposed, to see all the faces craning forward ecstatically. Gabrielle threw her arms around me. But next morning as migraine spread hot fingers over my face and skull I thought, what was that about? And I started to hate John. I accepted this hatred by small degrees until it resided in me, steady and deep.

I began to notice things, for example the lack of food. Usually I eat hugely. Seasickness has ruined my appetite, but there still isn't enough for me, and surely insufficient for the children. Not that we saw them after the first two weeks. They stayed in part of the ship out of bounds to adults. And the drudgery, hours of scrubbing, scouring and polishing, long after everything's spotless. I don't object to dirt or menial chores, I've done enough student jobs, and something in me quietens when I perform actions again and again. Yet these tasks are futile, exhausting, repeated until our hands are raw. Lights out at eleven, up again at four. Though I don't mind the nights. That's our time, Gabby's and mine. My bunk is plenty big enough, we lie so tightly in each other's arms. At night, hearing the suck and pull of the sea against the cabin wall I think, we'll be all right. Perhaps there's meaning in it all. When we arrive it will become clear.

Yet when day breaks, I know there's something strange and hard at the heart of this venture. Watching the meetings like a film, I understand what John is doing. One after another he directs his attention at the girls, the youngest first. He has them lined up in rows. His eyes, pale grey circles, are fixed on someone for a few evenings and always they get up and follow him out.

My prayers now are shrivelled things. 'Get us out. Please get us out.'

Gabrielle is slipping away. Distracted and distant, she doesn't pounce on me in corridors any more. The only time I reach her is when we make love.

I say, "Gabrielle, look at me," and hold her gaze. "Look at me," until she sees me. "Look at me, Gabby," as she dissolves and her body arches, her eyes mist and she murmurs, "My darling, my darling."

For these moments alone I would stay on this boat forever.

I miss the children. They haven't been seen for weeks and I'm worried. Only Daisy roams the ship, a giggling anarchist. At the first meetings she would sit in the front row, lobbing paper cups at John. He'd continue to boom like a monotonous gong, pretending not to notice. The music was moronic — bland Sunday school words displayed on a screen while a ball bounded along like karaoke. A CCTV camera filmed us, projecting the faces of elated individuals onto the monitor. I didn't dare look at Gabby, kept my face in my hands, but felt her shudder with laughter each time a cup bounced off John's head.

Now disrespect and merriment are impossible. Daisy and I are the only ones who laugh. Rejected by the children's tutor, she's been forgotten. Never has a child loved the sound of her own voice so much. She shouts out every thought in her head.

"I'm hungry!" or "Boring!" but mostly, "I want my Dad. I want to go home."

At first kids laughed, seized her hands and danced around, or adults caught her up and swung her into the air, but now the children are nowhere to be seen and everyone is serious. When I meet Daisy in the corridors she puckers up for slobbery kisses while I smuggle food from my pocket to hers. Or we crouch and draw with a pencil stub on the white walls, too low down for anyone to notice, little faces made funny with beards and glasses and big noses.

Some nights I stand by the rails, the ship in darkness. The breeze is warm, unlike the wind that blew through the emptying city for months. Again I think, maybe we'll be all right. When we arrive at our destination Gabby and I will get married, but beyond that my imagination fails. I worry about Daisy, every cell of her body with its extra chromosome curved like a little half moon, and wonder how that splinter of protein lets her winkle love out of me like a pin. When we land I'll buy a newspaper and scribble on the faces: moustaches, warts and big ears to make her laugh.

The meeting tonight is special. For the first time in weeks, the children will attend. John says they're ready now. Our journey is nearly over. Last night I saw lights and the shadow of hills as we drew close to the land. Told to fast and pray in preparation, Gabby and I spent the day in our bunk. As we file into the meeting room, smiling girls offer us pills, and water in a paper cup. I secrete mine in my cheek and pocket the cup for Daisy to play with. Later I discreetly spit the tablets into a tissue.

I'm delighted to see the kids, though they seem subdued. The group sways, everyone holding out their arms. We sing baby songs as the ball bounds across the screen, over and over until the meaning rubs off like the face on an old coin. There's a smell of unwashed bodies and hair. My God, how thin we are. The girls all have twine through their belt loops to hold up their jeans. John is staring at Gabrielle. She's in the front row closest to him. He can't take his eyes off her, the bastard. My stomach lurches and drops because she's next.

One after another the kids are summoned to the front. John spreads his fingers on each child's head.

"Go! Get out of here Satan!"

They shudder and gasp, or fall to the floor and jerk, curling their arms into their chests. John stretches out his hands.

"See, they're possessed by the spirits of wild animals!"

Gabrielle turns round to me, shocked, and whispers, "What's going on?"

My little brother used to do it, in a temper or when he was hurt: pant so hard his face went blue and hands cramped like claws.

I whisper, "Did you take that stuff?"

She shakes her head and shows me the pills, crushed to paste in her palm. I bend double, as if struck by stomach cramps, and run past the smiling girls at the door with Gabby behind me.

I say, "We've got to get away."

"How?"

"We're nearly there, I've seen land. It's not too far. Trust me."

Now Daisy is beside us. She says, "Are you going home? Can I come too? I hate John. I want my dad."

"Daisy, can you swim?"

She shouts, "I'm a brilliant swimmer. Daddy says I can do anything. I'm as good as anyone else!"

We climb onto the rails. My head is pounding and when I look at Gabrielle she has a dazzling, heart stopping, Catherine-wheel halo made of all the colours I've never seen in my life. It isn't migraine; I swear it's the real thing. I just couldn't see it before. I turn to Daisy and she has one too.

I say, "Gabby, look at me."

Gabrielle stares like the first time. We look down as if from a multi-storey car park and have never seen anything so terrible: the dark water frothing and boiling, the cold black night all around.

I say, "Let's go!" and we hold hands.

"Pray for us, Daise."

Daisy yells, "Jesus help us!"

Gabrielle says, "Into your hands, Lord."

I am twelve, on the top diving board, and my big brother is shouting, "Jump Ryan, you can do it!" and because I want to be like him, I do.

I think, God protect us. I have them both by the hand, so tight I'll never let them go.

Daisy cries, "Daddy! Daddy!"

Gabby says, "Now and at the moment of our deaths —"

We are falling. We are flying. My stomach soars up like a swing and my head explodes with coloured light and the water froths dark and I've never seen anything so terrible.

And the sea arches up.

The sea arches up to us.

Reaches out to catch us like the hand of God.

A GOOD MATCH

Siddique didn't mean to hit her. He had no idea where the blow came from. As wheals rose on her cheek and tears sprang to her eyes, he froze. Then he fled the bedroom, past his little niece cowering on the stairs because she'd seen everything. That night, Safia lay limp and silent beside him. Next morning there was a strange, rigid brightness in her manner as she left the house. When he phoned her mobile, it was switched off.

In an over-crowded house Siddique was lonelier than ever before. Two of his relatives never went out: his mother-in-law, motionless on the sofa with an indefinite sickness; his sister-in-law Nabeela, placidly performing her endless chores. He'd always looked forward to the times when his niece returned from nursery and they would watch T.V together. He laughed when the little girl laughed, ashamed he couldn't understand the cartoons and brightly-coloured talking animals. Now she huddled on the far side of the sofa, her shoulders and knees turned away. At least the child's jumbling mix of Leeds and Urdu was comprehensible. His wife would only speak in measured English now, avoiding his eyes.

Every day was the same. Safia went to work and came home, her mood level and blank as her face. At mosque he felt distant and dislocated, and there seemed little point going anymore. In the quiet places where his life should be joined, brackets were pulling apart.

He spent hours on their bed fantasising about Safia. Or he left the house and wandered the streets. Drawn to teenagers in short skirts, he would find himself at the secondary school. Even the Asian schoolgirls in traditional dress seemed exotic, with their confident movements and sexy headscarves. If they caught him staring they would throw him that look, so English and unfamiliar — a woman's disdain. Then he would feel again the stinging heat on his palm when he struck his wife. One-two: the flat of his hand, the back of his hand, as his father slapped his mother because a meal was over-cooked or a shirt scorch-marked. He used to watch from behind a door or across a table, afraid to speak or breathe, while everything slowed down and burned because he was just a child and this man was his father.

For years his parents had talked of his cousin Safia, a suitable match. They met once or twice on her infrequent holidays in Pakistan. Siddique barely understood her oddly accented Urdu, or she his stumbling English. She was foreign and uneasy in his dusty village, an awkward girl, not beautiful. His father said it would be a good marriage, hold the family together and settle debts. But these days, the new way, the girls from England had the final choice.

His mother said, "She'll want you, Siddique. You're the best looking."

When they were both twenty, she came over for three weeks. As his mother predicted, she chose him from three proffered cousins. Their wedding was a smudged canvas of colour and ritual. That night, both shy to undress and cling, they barely spoke. His brother had told him what to expect. She was soft and delicate beneath her clothes and it happened naturally, as his brother said. But so fast. The astonishing explosion of sensation was over before he could kiss his new wife.

They were apart for a year while immigration matters were organised and a visa arranged. On the phone she chatted but he had little to say. He couldn't picture her life in the city, her job as teaching assistant, or the house he would share with his in-laws. Everyone told him he was lucky. A future in England was better than sawing wood in his uncle's workshop, each day the same as the last.

He never thought it would be like this, hadn't imagined such loneliness and yearning for home. His previous existence seemed a far-away festival. He missed his job: the warm wood and weighty tools, the satisfaction as a piece of furniture came together. He pined for the conversation of men, and football after work. Now his days were spent with his chronically ill mother-in-law, who regained strength when the younger women left the house. And he distrusted Safia's sly, superior brother, Ramzan.

"Don't go out in those pyjamas Sid, you look like a peasant. Get some decent clothes," Ramzan said.

Safia brought home jeans and shirts she selected like a mother clothes for a child. In Pakistan Siddique never looked in mirrors; now he barely recognised himself. In the early days, when they'd go to the bedroom and make love as soon as she came home from work, Safia said he looked like a film star. He'd daydream about it before and after, and wondered if she felt the same. Did she think of him at school as she helped a child with coat or drawing? Or once she closed the front door, did she forget him?

Ramzan had a girlfriend. They kissed on the street, while Nabeela padded around indoors, cooking and cleaning. All English girls, with their brittle yellow hair and rolls of chubby midriff, looked the same to Siddique. He couldn't guess their ages. The girlfriend phoned the house and even came to the door.

Siddique said to Nabeela, "Don't you mind?"

"He's my husband," she said. "What can I do? If I go home I'd have to leave the children behind."

He looked at her closely. Although she cooked all day and her scolding mother-in-law piled her plate, she never seemed to eat. Hollow-eyed, wrists brittle as sticks, she starved as she prepared meals for a house full of people.

Siddique and Safia were happy at first. Surely they were. He called her mobile many times a day. He couldn't help it; she was always on his mind. Yet something was missing. Why wasn't she lost in him, as he was in her?

"I have to turn the phone off at school," she said. "I can't let it ring in the classroom."

She worked with a teacher named Phil.

"It's normal for men and women to work together. It's not a big deal."

She didn't cover her hair. Siddique wondered whether the teacher liked to imagine her naked. One day he followed her to school and waited outside. At break-time the children ran out. Safia and Phil walked across the playground to a shed. As they unpacked play equipment they looked relaxed, like a couple, and she laughed in a way he'd never heard, glancing up at Phil who smiled back as if they were touching. A quick cold blade passed through Siddique. He went home and waited.

"Phil says –"

She seemed excited, breathless.

"You were laughing together. I saw you," Siddique said.

"He's a funny guy. He makes me laugh."

He began to talk jerkily, as if his thoughts and words had unshackled.

"Do you want to have sex with him?"

"Don't be pathetic. You've got sex on the brain."

"You must give up that job. Never see him again."

She laughed then. Gave him that look. He hit her, one-two. The sound went on reverberating, his hand continued to burn, even as he fled the room and down the stairs. He heard the bed creak as she sat down hard. He had to get out before the tears came: hers, his.

Sex on the brain. It was true, she'd infected him. The women he passed on the street were wanton and cold. They didn't care. No father or brother could control them. He hung around the secondary school gates though the girls talked about him now. For a few minutes he'd follow them, then slip away. Their looks and whispers were dangerous, but he couldn't stop. Cruel fantasies slid unbidden into his head as if Satan had entered through an eyeball and was slithering between his ears. When Siddique was twelve, two men from the village got hold of a low-caste girl. They hit her, one-two, and held her down in the dirt. Snot, tears and blood ran down her face. Siddique and his brother watched from behind a wall.

Afterwards his brother said, "She's a wicked girl, she was begging for it. She sinned."

But Siddique knew why she was begging. And she'd seen him; her eyes had met his with fear and hatred as if he was one of them.

She disappeared from the village and no one mentioned her again. The men swaggered around, and attended mosque as though nothing had happened. Siddique's skin changed temperature whenever he thought of it. The mind makes chains and hooks — one image snares another. Sometimes in dreams he was her, other times them. They embodied everything that frightened him and all he was capable of.

Ramzan said, "Listen Taliban, hit my sister again and I'll kill you."

But Siddique had seen bruises on Nabeela's face.

One day Nabeela collected the children from school and nursery and didn't come back. The freezer was full of meals she'd spent weeks preparing. Spaces and shadows appeared that Siddique hadn't noticed before. How had such a quiet person filled the house? He remembered all the hours he'd spent with her, another man's wife. He would lean against the sink talking as she ground spices or emptied the washing machine, and Nabeela would reply carefully as if his every comment warranted deliberation. Ramzan sulked, complaining of dirty shirts and rings around the bath until his mother dragged herself from the sofa. About his missing wife and children, he said nothing.

"Is she coming back?" Siddique asked.

"Not if she's got any sense," said Safia.

"Where is she?"

"At a refuge. The doctor arranged it."

"What's that?"

"A secret place women go to escape violent men."

A thin film of calm around her kept him out.

For a moment he thought he could hold everything in. But suddenly he was sobbing like no man should in front of a woman, making noises he'd never heard before. She stared, shocked, then reached out and held his arm as he sat shuddering on the bed, the first time she'd touched him for weeks.

"The doctor said after they hit you once they always do it again," she said.

She was crying too.

"What's the doctor got to do with it?" Siddique said.

"I took Nabeela to the G.P. She had to get away."

"I'm not like your brother. You know I'm not."

"Why don't you get it?" Safia said. "Phil's just a bloke at work. He's years older than us, with three little kids."

"Safia, there's something wrong with me, like a sickness inside."

She was lying next to him now.

"You're homesick, that's all," she said.

He felt the heat of her all down one side.

"Things will get better." Her voice became sing-song. "Why don't you listen? Phil says his brother would give you a job. He fits kitchens and needs someone to help with the carpentry."

"I won't take anything from that man."

"It's not a favour. It's a job. And you could go to college in the evenings. Improve your English."

"I'll never do it again. I swear I won't. I promise," Siddique said.

She was laughing and crying as she undid his buttons. Her arms around him inside his shirt were sweeter than any fantasy.

SHUTTERS

I ordered the metal blinds from an industrial supplier. The fitter seemed amused.

"Expecting nuclear war, mate? Know something we don't?"

I said, "Crime round here. My wife's not well."

It took days to get rid of the stench of his cheap deodorant. Not that I allowed him in the house for long. I cleaned his imprint from the sills and windows with bleach.

Is anyone ever really safe, Rose, once they set eyes on what they want?

It's been a bad day. My mind is still churning. The shutters rolled down over every door and window muffle the sounds of the city. The one on our bedroom window is skew, letting a triangle of moonlight fall on the lino. In the morning I'll mend it. You used to insist we raise them during the day, but for months you haven't complained. I've checked the outside of the house and drawn the bolts on each door. As always I showered and scrubbed my fingernails before bed. The bedroom I disinfected earlier. Since I removed the carpet and curtains that collected dust mites, it's easier. You disliked the plastic sheets at first, but now you agree that with your difficulties, they're more hygienic. And as you know, I prefer a simple life.

You wouldn't like me to lower my standards. There's no point cleaning a room, just to pollute it with germs and body odours. Remember when Sheila was little and I'd wash her in a bowl outside before allowing her into the house? You fretted about her catching cold, until I fixed up the shower in the cupboard by the back door. If she'd brought friends home it might have been awkward, but she didn't seem to have any. She preferred to spend time in her bedroom. Teenagers are like that.

Not that I trusted her. She was sly. When I checked the carpet pile to see if she'd entered the living room without permission, sometimes I found it disturbed. After she left home she wrote letters to you behind my back. When you became ill I found the false compartment in your underwear drawer. Carpentry and deceit are beyond you, Rose: Sheila was responsible, of course. I check our mail, so you must have had her letters delivered elsewhere. And still you won't explain.

"She's our daughter, Andre."

After Sheila left home she became unreal, an abstraction. I was happy to be just two again.

It's been a year since you said, "There's something wrong with me. I ought to see the doctor."

Why say things like that? My skin went hot and cold. You look knock-out. You've lost weight, but it suits you. We don't need doctors. Better you avoid those smug bastards with E.coli under their fingernails, and that mucky, MRSA ridden hospital. You know I'm right. The blinds stay closed so the neighbours don't interfere. I look after you, Rose. Like any ex-soldier, I'm not squeamish and know the importance of hygiene.

Yet you seem quiet. At your age a woman's body alters; lately your belly has filled up. Sometimes you ask for Sheila.

"Great daughter," I remind you. "Where is she? I was right, wasn't I? Bad blood, that girl."

You always stuck up for her, even when she was sixteen and ran off with that black man. After everything I'd taught her, the little tart.

"He's mixed race — so what?" you said. "And he's not a man, he's seventeen. A really nice boy."

"Nice boy, my arse. Screwing my daughter in secret. She knows nothing. She'd let anyone do it and ask questions later."

"Why do you have to go on like that? They're just kids. Why can't you let her be happy?"

You met him without telling me. When you look at me like that I can't stand it, Rose. Don't shut me out.

You're too open. People confide in you, spilling their troubles for you to sponge up. You used to blab about new friends endlessly, as if each time it might last. I'd let it go on for a year or two, accompanying you on nights out. I can be charming when I want. The men were irrelevant, all boring as hell, but the women gave you something. We rarely laugh, but with them you were hilarious. Those god-awful evenings with other couples, you so giddy and eager, it made me cringe.

I'd watch those women carefully for the first hint of rejection.

"God, what a snide comment. Didn't you notice? She'll hurt you Rose, like they all do."

Lives are meant to be separate and apart. Believe me, if the borders break and spill over, only trouble results. They continued to phone even after I called a halt. Not wanting you upset, I intercepted the calls and letters. A year might pass before they got the hint.

Once the friendships were finished, I shredded the photos.

Now you're ill it's better. There's only me. Lying beside you on the plastic sheet, I tell you things I never could before. I realised you were a good listener the first time we met in the pub in Earls Court. Remember, Rose? I'd been in the country only a few weeks, and you were working as a chambermaid in that big hotel. When you told me you'd left your town up north to see the world, I had to laugh. You were so beautiful I couldn't believe my luck. After we went back to my room that Saturday you never returned to work.

On the Friday I said, "Put your best dress on girl, we're getting married."

Thirty seven years ago, our anniversary next week. I haven't forgotten.

It wasn't just for the passport. I fell for you. I'll never desert you, or let you go. That time I came home early and you were packing a bag, I thought you were leaving me. I made you explain — you were just going to visit your sister. You promised never to see her again. And those other times Rose; I don't like to think of them now. I'm not proud of my actions, but I was beside myself. I love you so much.

Before you I had my share of women. I made no secret of it, did I? Most are so vain they'll do anything if you feign interest. No girl rejected me. When she was attached and getting dull, I'd ditch her. No reasons, so she apologised, pleaded and blamed herself. When I was twelve and my father left, I did the same. All those calls from a phone box to say, 'I miss you, Dad.' He'd promise to come for me, but never show. I wrote letters, making amends for nothing, which he didn't answer. It seems pathetic now. The sunnier a girlfriend's disposition, the less touched by disappointment and cynicism, the greater my satisfaction. I'd think, so now she knows.

With you it was different. I hate to see you suffer. But it's not too bad, is it? This year has been peaceful, reminding me of my time in the desert in the army. Picture the two of us sleeping out on the other side of the earth, watching stars dissolve in inky space. Over here the stars are diminished and tame, arranged in unconvincing ploughs and bears, glimpsed occasionally through cloud. I like to think of the desert, untouched and empty, cleansed endlessly by wind and sun. Gravel grey mountains, every cleft and crease naked, folding back and back to a sky white as bread. In bed I feel us floating, as if in the canoes my platoon requisitioned. I imagine you well again, paddling with me down a river that cuts its way through rock, while birds dive and break the water like shattering a mirror.

The desert is beautiful. You must eat and get strong, and when you're better I'll take you there. Where did the years go, Rose? I only wanted you to be happy.

The commotion this evening must have disturbed you. So bloody inconsiderate. Through the peep-hole in the front door I saw two men in suits and a plump, dowdy middle aged woman. The banging went on for some time. The phone rang, moaning into the air. Footsteps circled the house. I smiled, knowing I'd left no window unshuttered.

121

"Mr Swart, it's the doctor. Please let me in. Your daughter is very worried and thinks your wife needs medical attention."

Sheila? That slob on the step? After twenty years I didn't recognise her.

"Please be reasonable. Our only concern is to help your wife."

Standing quietly behind the door, I listened to them mutter to each other.

"There's a social worker here too, Mr Swart. We have powers under the mental health act. If you won't let us in, we can instruct the police to force entry. We believe your wife is seriously ill."

Three locks, two bolts. Leaving the chain on, I pushed the door open slightly. The fat woman was in tears; a cracking, sliding look on her face. After all these years our daughter betrayed us.

Sheila said, "Just let the doctor in for God's sake. There are some things you can't control."

Refusing to look at her, I unhooked the chain for the doctor. The others tried to enter, but I stood across the doorway, then locked the door behind him leaving them outside.

His shoes were so loud on the floorboards as I followed him upstairs, I wished I'd made him take them off. I felt myself emptying faster and faster, like water from an unplugged bath. The doctor looked round the bedroom thoughtfully, impressed by the cleanliness, his vile hospital shamed. Without even washing his hands he took things from his bag. Checked your blood pressure and chest, and pulled down the sheet to prod your belly. Your unsociability surprised me. Usually you perk up and prattle at a new face. I was glad you saw through someone for once.

"I'll speak to the consultant and get her admitted straight onto the ward. I don't want her hanging around in accident and emergency."

Sitting on our bed, he turned his shoulders away and mumbled into a mobile phone. He still hadn't taken off his coat. I imagined all the disgusting places it had been.

"Bed bureau say the waiting time is four hours for admissions. She'll be okay until then. They'll send an ambulance. You can get a bag ready for her."

Saying nothing, biding your time, you didn't commit yourself. Good girl, I thought. We'll laugh about the pompous prat later.

"I know this is difficult, Mr Swart. You've done your best, but you must let someone else take responsibility now."

The doctor held out his hand. After a second it fell to his side and he packed his bag.

"I'm afraid you don't see the situation clearly." His voice was stripped.

All that time I'd not spoken a word. I couldn't. A weight was breaking my ribs.

Four hours. Clean again, stretched out beside you, I feel calmer. I imagine sand beneath us, stars like pinholes and the moon a blue marble. The desert night is cold, but we're fine with each other for warmth. There's so much I still need to tell you, Rose. You paid so much attention to other people's blather, there was never enough time for me. Although you don't answer, you understand. Listen: that stuff with the village women in the desert. War is war, and sex means nothing to them. They get over it. It was nothing to Sheila either, nothing at all, even at thirteen. You wouldn't listen when I told you she'd do it with anyone. Believe me, I know. With you it was different. That was love.

You'll be all right, I promise. No doctor will open you up in a filthy operating theatre. They can't take you away — you're mine. In the army I learned techniques I guessed might be useful again one day. Actions that cut trenches in my brain and nerves and fingers, so deep I never forgot.

Like I said, no one is safe once they set eyes on what they want. You were all I ever wanted, Rose. Things don't take the shape we expect; there's never the ending we imagine. But Sheila was wrong as always. This I can control.

LOVE ON THE ROCKS

Tim pauses as they pass a small rocky beach.

"Remember this place?"

Trailing his paddle in the water, he nods towards the shore and grins at Eve over his shoulder. Dawn still mists the horizon like a breath. The white edged mountains remind Eve that twenty years ago she thought, 'Snow! In the Mediterranean!' Until they drew close enough to distinguish the whitewashed houses clinging to the crags. The islands have changed since then. Cars replace donkeys, and the beach-sleeping hippies have grown up and gone. The scent of rosemary remains, and the constant, slurring sea.

At first she doesn't remember. They let the kayak drift. Morning sounds float from the island: a radio's gabble, barking, the lament of goats. Then all at once, vivid as the sun's flare on the retina, she pictures their young selves. She hadn't recognised the cove from all those they passed. How could she forget? The years unwind and she remembers how they yanked impatiently at the clothes that separated them. She recalls the smell of his skin, feels again his hand on her breast and sand grazing her thighs. Later, examining the abrasions and rock imprints on each other's bodies, they couldn't help laughing.

As he smirks at her over his shoulder she laughs again, reminded of the passion still stored at the heart of their feeling for each other. What could be more absurd and beautiful than swaying in a kayak a few yards from where they made love twenty years before? She wishes she could remember every time. She watches the muscles of his forearms as he twists the paddles, the hands that with delicate precision have her body's measure. She thinks of his mouth that knows where to kiss, and when to stop kissing. They are printed on each other like two halves of a mould.

They set off again, leaving the beach behind. She watches his back and shoulders move beneath his tee shirt. With a small pang she notes new creases on his neck, and the vulnerable thin patch on his crown he can't see. Pulling a sunhat from his back pocket, she reaches up and slips it onto his head.

After an hour they reach the cave. As they enter, the air cools and the water changes from indigo to emerald to black. At first there is only religious darkness. Through dappled light she makes out walls stained green by centuries of slime and seepage. The high ceiling is deformed with warty outgrowths that heave, break off and skitter around, making tiny urgent sounds she at first struggles to hear. As her retinas adjust she sees mouths open and close in mournful teddy bear faces, and a multitude of pin-point eyes. Bats paper the cave. Some hang nonchalantly from one long crooked finger. They let go, plummet and swoop up again. Others flitter from ledge to crack, or sleep wrapped in their wings like a bag lady's coat. The squeaks and clicks quieten at the echoey splash of the paddles. Thousands of pointed ears listen in the darkness and Eve, too, strains to catch sounds just beyond reach.

They lie down in the kayak and the world floats away. Stippled in jade light, she stretches along Tim, her thigh over his. Her breathing changes. Pushing up her shirt, he strokes her breast under her swimsuit, the curve of waist and hip. Light as a wasp, his hand comes to rest between her legs. She wriggles free and sits astride his thighs, tugging up his tee shirt to kiss his belly. He lifts his arms, smiling, as she pulls his shirt off, rolls it up and places it beneath his head.

"What are you up to?" he says.

A dragonfly dances inside her. Skipping her hand across the front of his swimming trunks she delights at her effect on him. She kisses along his waist band and slips a hand inside, caressing soft skin above wiry hair, pulling down his trunks to take him in her mouth. His musky scent mixes with the taste of seawater. He sighs and the kayak rocks with each shift of their weight.

Her tongue on the place he likes best, she lets the swell of the sea work for her, for him. She cradles his testicles in a familiar conspiracy. He makes a glottal exclamation and before she can understand, the movement has tipped them out. Icy water slides over her like mouths and hands; her chest tightens so she can hardly breathe. They tread water, nonplussed and hilarious. Then he's swimming, holding her shoulders as he guides her backwards onto a submerged rocky shelf. Her stomach plunges as he pulls off her swimming costume. Their bodies gleam white-green in the half light, strange and slippery as mermaids. Wavelets suck her breasts and hips. Concentric ripples of pleasure spread. His heat reaches her, unfamiliar through cold water, his mouth warm on hers. Knotted together in an old embrace, they row their boat off the edge of the world.

The kayak has floated to the other side of the cave and its retrieval takes effort. They climb back in and lie curled around each other, looking up at the shifting leathery blanket of bats. Their skin dries in the swarming air. Her discarded swimming costume has disappeared. His knee is badly scratched. Eve thinks, he hasn't changed. Through all these years he has been revealed to me.

Presently they start to shiver. The bat smell is soupy and overpowering.

"Shall we go?"

They dress, then pushing the paddles against rocks, manoeuvre their way out of the cave. Space and heat crash down from the sky; the world outside is dense and clear. She hands him his sun hat.

They are tired, aching and the journey back against the wind will be harder. Passing the secluded beach, they'll exchange smiles. They will see many things and thread more beads on this life they have strung together. Yet Eve understands that in time one of them will falter. Despite his broad shoulders and middle aged vitality, she suspects this will be Tim. She will paddle for both of them, but one day, he will slip away from her into the waves and she'll carry on alone. The shore will never look any closer. Later still she will lay her paddle aside. Sliding into the water's caress, she will duck down and swim to him through all the space, untouched and beautiful, that lies beneath sea and sky.

MERCY IS SICK TODAY

Mercy is sick today. She was sick yesterday and the day
before that, but tomorrow will be better. An old woman
gave me medicine from the bush. I boiled the herbs to juice
and made my sister drink. Last week Mercy returned from
the city. Wrapped in her chitenge, she lies on a straw mat
outside the hut. Her forehead shines and sweat darkens
her blouse. Flicking at flies, shooing curious children, I
guard her. At midday I light the fire for nsima. Not everyone
in the village will eat today. Fearing a neighbour's jealous
magic, I take care not to clatter the cooking pot. As the
water simmers I picture my sister's altered face in the
troubled surface. Taking the bucket I walk half an hour to
the tap, wait my turn and fetch water to bathe her.

The women ask, "What's wrong with Mercy?"

"She's tired from the journey," I say. "Resting. Tomorrow
she'll get up and tell us about everything — her job and
husband and house."

As I bathe her, dipping and wringing the cloth, I sing
our mother's songs. Strange blotches spoil her skin. Mercy
joins in softly. I'm pleased that after all these years she
remembers the words.

Now as she sleeps, I wonder. Seven years ago she
walked away from the village and our father's anger. When
she woke me that night, wearing her Sunday dress with
spare clothes in a bundle, I barely understood — I was only
a child. She whispered urgently about a trucker who had
passed through and sent for her to join him. She hated to
leave me, but loved him and had to go.

129

"I'll write and send money every month," Mercy said. "When you're older, you can come too. We'll live together in the city. You'll go to a proper school, and when you know everything, you can paint your nails red and work behind the desk in a big hotel."

The letters and money never came. Every day I thought of my sister as I hacked the cracked earth before school or stood in line at the water tap. In the dusty school room, singing out times-tables as the sun poured through the open door, she was with me. A new baby came for Mother every spring. When Father died I hoped Mercy would come home, but didn't know how to reach her. Each year was harder than the last. Neighbours helped with a cup of sugar or an egg for the baby, but had little to share.

When my first bleed came, Mother said I must stop school. Boys began to watch me on my way to the field. I dreamed of Mercy, dancing in high heels or drinking tea at a glass table. Her nails were red and she was always laughing.

Then she came home, as everyone does at last. Having eaten city fruit, they return with sunken bellies and wasted arms. Mother braids my sister's hair and cries a little. We haven't mentioned her truck driver. I want to hear about the wedding, but am scared to say his name. Tomorrow she will get up, eat and tell me everything. But today Mercy is sick and we lie on the mat with our arms around each other, staring dark into dark.

THE SPACES BETWEEN

Rain fell for weeks from a low metallic sky. As I drove to work and home again, separated from the city by the warmth and music inside the car, I began to notice changes in the half-light. Streets that used to empty at dusk had taken on the expectant, temporary air of a railway station. Every evening people and their belongings cluttered the pavements, yet by morning they'd gone. There were children everywhere, inadequately dressed, sly and darting as squirrels.

People began to camp in the surgery car park under plastic sheets and tarpaulins. The police moved them on, but most mornings I shifted bags and boxes from my parking space. So when a small figure left the damp huddle of children by the wall and headed for me, I was wary.

"Good morning, Dr Susan Campbell. How are you?"

He extended a clammy hand. The unexpected formality made me smile. The lilt and courtesy were familiar. Without thinking I touched my right forearm with left index finger as we shook hands — an African civility I hadn't used for twelve years.

"Doctor, I am William Matemba's son. My name is Geoffrey. How are you going to help me?"

Rainwater streamed from his bin liner cape into a puddle around his flip-flops. William's son? I remembered a shiny solemn toddler, riding his father's shoulders, holding his ears. But why here, twelve years older, bone thin and looking as if he hadn't washed for weeks?

"What are you doing here?" I asked.

"My aunt got money and sent me. She wanted me to get away. She told me to find you. You would help me."

He grinned.

"I have to work today," I said.

A small queue of regulars at the locked surgery door watched with guarded curiosity from beneath their umbrellas.

"Find me again later and we'll talk."

The thought of Geoffrey snagged during the day, but I'd no time for reflection. Recently an unprecedented number of new patients, from all over the world, had joined the list. Many were children, twelve or thirteen years old. There seemed no pattern to their stories. Our new patients seemed content to shelter aimlessly in the surgery for hours. They brought the wet in. The waiting room pulsed with young voices.

Having few interests outside work, I spent the evenings looking for clues. The newspapers, obsessed with celebrities and diets, didn't help. Wars and famines were deemed random, barely relevant events. The local paper reported the unusual weather at length, but failed to mention the refugees. I searched news sites, but couldn't piece together a credible explanation. I began to doubt myself. Had I really seen children on the roofs of derelict buildings, or did the driving rain deceive me? Were the adolescents with bundles any different from those who loiter on the streets of any city? Yet something was different. The receptionists noticed.

"Most of these kids don't have anyone with them. Nobody has a passport or papers at all."

Parents were getting their children out, the older ones, able to fend for themselves, first. As if from a rising flood, an informal worldwide evacuation was taking place.

Geoffrey Matemba must be thirteen or fourteen, but was tiny enough to pass for nine, as if he'd not eaten enough throughout his childhood. His father had been a stocky man. Remembering how much William loved his little son, a dart of sadness pierced me.

I took Geoffrey home. What else could I do? He had nothing with him. I couldn't imagine how he'd survived the weeks before he found me. He became quiet and drowsy in the warmth of the car, gazing out at the clouds that hung like rags from a dirty sky.

I said, "It's not like the rain in Africa."

Glancing at Geoffrey in the failing light, I saw his father's likeness in cheekbone and brow. Memory settled like dust. When the first rains fell on the tin roof of the hospital, we had to shout above the din. Stepping outside was like walking through a warm waterfall, we were drenched so fast. Next day the waterlogged red earth was heavy with life. Everything steamed and swarmed. Even fence posts began to grow green leaves. As if whisked up from the mud, huge moths appeared and stuck like furry pancakes to the walls. I remembered surveying the empty hospital the morning after the rains came. The previous day the wards had been so full that patients slept on straw mats in the corridors. Now everyone, no matter how ill, had gone. They had to start planting if their families were to eat next year.

In the battered Land Rover, grinding through red mud to a health centre, William Matemba turned to me.

"It wasn't like this before. Something's changed. There's so much illness and the rains used to be better. There were never so many hungry children. What's happening to the world?"

It was his world, not mine — alien and disorientating as another planet. I'd been there two years and had nothing to compare. Only the human body was familiar, suffering and anguish the same. Maybe he was talking about a change in himself, not the world. His wife had died the previous year of the unnameable wasting disease that was picking off the health staff, one by one.

We used to talk a lot in the Land Rover. William Matemba was the public health inspector and accompanied me on weekly visits to the health centres. I liked him. Sardonic and compassionate, he made sense of things. Only he knew how shamefully I felt my limitations. At the health centres — isolated shacks staffed by alcoholic or depressed medical assistants — he checked supplies of kerosene and vaccines while I saw patients. Never had I been so ill equipped to help.

I should have been honoured to be the first he told about his scholarship. He came to my house, a little whitewashed building with concrete floors and cockroaches in every crack and keyhole. Every evening when the generator and electricity clicked off at nine o'clock, I could barely stand it. He talked about work and his baby boy, but couldn't contain himself long.

"I'll be in England for two years, starting next October, after you get home."

He would leave Geoffrey with his sister. He hated to part from him but it was a great chance for them both. Even as a student he would earn far more than here. He couldn't wait to leave this country where you struggled to earn enough to buy your child shoes.

"Maybe, after my course, I'll find a job in England. Then Geoffrey will have a future."

He used my Christian name for the first time. "Susan, when I'm over there, perhaps we could meet. May I visit you? I'd like to see where you work."

Beneath his reserve was a ringing tension. I knew this was the first good thing since his wife died. Yet I hesitated, just for a second. Actions and words change things, but so do the spaces between. Events that transform life can be invisible. When I wake at night or get into my car to drive home, I still think of that silence, brief as a heartbeat, and all it contained: for him, for me. I'd imagined him in England, in his shabby suit that smelled faintly of wood smoke and disinfectant, and couldn't picture us together.

I said quickly, "That would be nice. I'll give you my address."

But it was too late. You can't withdraw silence. It gives nothing back.

"Dr Campbell, I didn't mean —"

His face reduced to a puzzle of bone and shadow.

"Of course not."

Afterwards it was different between us. He stayed in the back of the Land Rover with the other staff. When he sat with me he was polite, but our conversations had hollowed out. We didn't laugh together any more. It saddened me, but my contract was nearly over. I was going home.

I heard what happened from the hospital matron. For a while she and I exchanged Christmas cards and courteous letters filled with good will to family members never met, or in my case that didn't exist. But hers were a litany of deaths. My old colleagues were dying, one by one. I couldn't imagine who would replace them.

'*Mr Matemba went to England for his studies,*' Matron wrote. '*I'm sorry to tell you he soon became very ill, was admitted to hospital and died. Mr Matemba was a good man, but such is God's will.*'

Sitting on the stairs with Matron's letter in my hand I thought, if only I'd reached out, touched his arm and said, 'William, that would be great!' everything could have been different. If we'd met I'd have noticed his failing health and made him seek help. Treatment is better here. He might have lived. I could have shown him where I worked, taken him places, explained England to him as he had Malawi to me. He needn't have died alone in a strange cold place he didn't understand.

The terrible calculations of regret.

Now I stand in the hall with William's son. The small space fills with his damp, pungent smell. Geoffrey necks around at my modest, sparsely furnished semi.

"Is all this yours? Do you live here by yourself? And there's an upstairs also?"

He's delighted there's an upstairs. It's absurd, I agree — all this for one person. When I show him the box room he's pleased. I picture us making a boy's room, with skateboard posters and a desk for homework. In my living room, dwarfed on the sofa, he clasps a mug of hot chocolate and seems to vibrate with hidden electricity. His skin is inflamed and there are orange patches in his hair. I imagine the good food I'll give him. Of course he must go to school. Should I let social services know? Officially this child without papers doesn't exist.

Geoffrey says, "Dr Campbell?"

"Call me Susan. Your father did."

"Susan, I'm glad your house is so big. There's room for my wife."

A shuddering hysteria starts up in me.

"Your wife? How old is she?"

"She doesn't know. About eleven."

"I'll get bunk beds," I say.

From his end of the sofa, Geoffrey tentatively extends a leg until his foot, curved like a little seahorse, rests against me. My fingers trace vein and tendon, the thick cracked sole. Rain against the window shutters us in.

He says, "Does it ever stop raining here?"

"In the end."

"At home the rains didn't come for three years."

"I know. It isn't fair."

Extinguished by fatigue, he's asleep. I gently move his foot and stand at the window, reminded of all the unfinished conversations in my life. The city widens around us. Somewhere a little girl crouches beside a wheelie bin beneath a plastic bag cape. When he wakes, we'll go out and find her. Between us lies only a dark space filled with rain.

FAIRY STORY

Between the turn of the handle and the door swinging
open I wonder, will she ever get out? Twice a week I catch
three buses across the city to see her. In six months I've
never failed. The evenings before are spent cooking treats.
She loves food. I remember chocolate pudding smeared on
her high chair; ice creams big as a toddler's head; her first
surprised mouthful of curry.

The nurse accepts my offerings without comment. Once
she took me aside and said, "Kate, in our experience this
doesn't work. She won't take anything from you. Be
patient."

Hoping the staff are hungry during breaks, I leave the
food there. I hate to see it wasted.

Lisa lies curled on her bed like a sick kitten. Through
half open doors I spot other girls who have put their lives
on hold. Wraiths drift through the unit; others watch TV or
study as if in a role-play of normal young adulthood.
Teenage fashions parody their freakish bodies: loose jeans
dip below scooped-out bellies, knotted spines press
through sequinned fabric. My daughter's back is covered
with fine fur. Having regressed through all the stages of
childhood, her body is infantile. At birth she was like a
blond monkey, but the white down that covered her then
rubbed off with baby oil within a few weeks.

I never know what to expect. Sometimes Lisa seems
pleased to see me and we talk of friends and schoolwork,
although her room shows few signs of meaningful activity.
My fridge is covered with paper scraps on which I've jotted

down things I must remember to tell her — funny or awkward incidents to make her laugh. Sometimes she smiles, but usually her expression is shuttered. When she was eight I could render her helpless with mirth. Sensitive as a cracked tooth and tormented by blushes, her one consolation then was that my life was more bedevilled by mishap than she imagined hers to be.

"Mum, did anything embarrassing happen to you today?"

She would listen with delight as I related blunders so absurd that her childish humiliations were trivial in comparison. And because I would have done anything to shield her from such feelings, I began to welcome these events, to collect and embellish them. There was no shortage of cringe making occasions. My life played out for her was a slow motion pratfall of toilet doors pulled open by strangers, public displays of underwear and unfortunate flatulence in solemn moments.

These incidents, real or embroidered, anchored me. The year Lisa was eight I was in a dream, unable to speak and slowly falling. Although I took my child to school and the park, and went to work at the call centre, I was rarely present. I was somewhere else — I can't explain it — in unknown back streets where my thoughts dodged and ducked. And my husband Kevin, who sensed but had no name for my distraction, couldn't call me back.

Some days Lisa wraps herself in her duvet and won't speak. Hard and secretive as a flick-knife, she turns on her side away from me.

The nurse says, "It's a bad day."

When I leave, the air outside is shameful sweet reprieve. Everything is bright and sharp. Life goes on — a dog sniffs a tree, boys kick a can. Treacherously alive, exhilarated to be free of her, I sing with relief. The bus driver smiles and I beam back, unable to believe my luck: I'm not her. And I think of everything I should have said.

Lately it's been difficult because I haven't been well. For the first time in my life I've been off work. This week I'll return to the doctor for the test results that will explain everything. Each day, different joints swell and ache. On waking I examine myself to find the place that will make my teeth grate today. I'm loaded with fatigue and slick with sweat. Warmth unfreezes my joints, so I lie in the bath until the water cools. As I examine my swollen wrist I remember that someone once turned my hand and kissed the palm. From my bath I watch the play of light through images of all that happened next. Memories I've avoided for ten years.

Because nothing is ever over. Time moves in waves and folds like water. Ten years ago all I could think of was Faye. Her eyes, her hands. I was falling in slow, dazzled motion. She was my first thought when I woke, the last at night. And Kevin's body that I'd loved so much seemed too thick and grossly muscular, its smells unwelcome, the contrast too great.

His leaving felt like this: severing, emptiness and ricocheting panic. With violet commas below her eyes, Lisa watched it all — my slip at the cliff edge, the ruinous descent, the splintering to pieces at the bottom. Had I acted differently, my daughter would not need now to starve herself to death. These are my thoughts in the bath as I gingerly move my grating joints. But mostly I think of Faye.

I hate to be off sick. Work fills up gaps and crevasses —
without it, brackish water trickles in like an underground
cave. At the call centre I have targets, and find it restful to
use words not my own. I must ask a question three times,
three different ways, before I can hang up. My calls are
monitored so I do this correctly. Within seconds I picture
the person on the other end of the line. Most are distracted
and irritable, but some are lonely and pleased to hear a
voice. Sometimes I sense disappointment as if they
expected someone else. Hope can fly up like a swing at the
phone's first vibration, even though the one you wait for
never rings.

Once a child's voice said, "My Nana won't wake up.
She's gone a funny colour."

Another time, "She's left me. The wardrobe's empty,
everything's gone."

But usually, "We don't want that. No thank you. Get off
the line please."

The phone calls began during my second week off work.
Grumbling, I heaved myself from the bath. The first time I
didn't recognise her voice.

She said, "Who can that be? Is Lisa alright?"

This was strange because the same words went through
my head as I limped downstairs. Then I realised the voice
was Faye's, as if ten years hadn't passed. Replacing the
receiver I wondered, did that happen? I dialled call-back
but the number was withheld.

The second time she said, "My knee hurts so much I
can't stand it."

Again it was like she read my mind. I remembered that
when we were together, it seemed she could. After that the

calls came regularly, many times an hour. I heard my thoughts expressed in Faye's voice — tediously repeated, or rephrased and from a different angle. She recounted half remembered dreams, and childhood incidents I'd never told anyone. Like something thrown at you with the sun in your eyes, I would sense a call coming. When my joints were most painful or I was languid with fever, her voice flew on my thoughts like kite-tails.

I wanted to talk like we used to.

I said, "Why did you leave? I can't be happy without you. I miss you."

And, "Did you hear about Lisa? What shall I do? I don't know how to put it right."

But replies came in my voice, or that of a past self, not hers. Each question had many answers and I didn't know which was true.

Once when the phone had rung all morning I said, "Where are you, Faye? My darling, are you alive?"

But there was only the dial tone.

At last the fever subsided. The walls no longer see-sawed when I moved my head. My joints cooled. The delicate boundary between sleep and waking shifted.

The doctor said, "Probably a virus. The tests were negative. It shouldn't happen again."

After weeks without appetite I'm starving and wake with food on my mind. One evening I cook Lisa a lasagne but after a moment's thought, eat it myself. I understand how hungry my daughter must be, the enormity of her self control.

The phone hasn't rung for two weeks.

Lisa says, "You're looking better, Mum."

I revel in my new found health and sharpened senses. In their infinite continuity of shading, colours seem more complex. Something calm and good has started up in me that I haven't felt for years.

Lisa says, "Who's Faye? Is she that old friend of yours? I keep getting calls on my mobile. They're so distorted I can't hear what she's saying."

I say, "Faye was someone in a book I once read. Long ago, maybe when I was a child. Switch your phone off, you don't have to answer. I'll tell you a fairy story."

To my surprise Lisa settles back expectantly against the pillows. Taking her hand, I trace the lilac lacework of veins.

I describe enchantment. You fall asleep for ten years, or a hundred, and wake to an altered world. I tell of food laced with magic. Fairies that spirit children away and return them changed. And if you step off the path, put your foot on the wrong stone, you can be drawn down into the ground by the weight of earth all around.

I say she must not be afraid.

Because there's always a way back. The good and courageous will prevail. And if you are lost, sooner or later someone you love will come and find you.

I read this long ago but still believe it to be true.

For the first time in years my little girl closes her eyes and allows me to stroke the hair from her forehead until she's asleep.

SALT MAN

The river rears over the bridge wall and surges onto the road. Rush-hour cars founder axle-deep in swirling sewage. Half submerged wheelie bins bob and circle, spewing their contents. Taken violently by the torrent, a traffic light rocks and topples.

On the pub wall a huge TV screen is tuned to the regional news. Every hour this evening I've watched the traffic light's slow-motion fall.

Rain flails the windows. The darkness outside is noise and destruction. From time to time the door opens. The wind roars and a customer blows in, stumbling over sandbags as bottles and glasses slide and rattle on the bar. The door slams shut with a jangling of bells.

The old man's hand on his glass is battered like a gardening glove.

He says, "Don't waste money on a hotel, pal. I've got a caravan in me yard. You can stay for nowt."

"I don't know," I reply. "I think I'm alright."

My fingers move a matchstick along the cribbage board. After so many years I'm surprised I can still play. Unable to get home, separated by the storm from my wife and daughter, I feel weightless. All roads out are impassable. It happened so fast, from travel warnings at lunch-time to the city ham-strung by five o'clock. For hours my mobile had no signal. Now when I ring home no one picks up.

"I tell you, if that caravan could talk. It's seen some times, believe me. Good job I never had a missus. You married?"

He has been drinking steadily all evening at my expense. I don't want to hear any more, but we're coupled by the storm. I murmur something, twisting my wedding ring beneath the table. Gemma forgets to secure the front door at night, believing her half-baked Karma will protect us. So far she's right, but fails to notice the chain lock I use on Karma's behalf. I wonder how I've let it happen. Why live so far out that I'm severed from my family by a day of rain? Admittedly on occasions it was convenient. Three times, in fact — surely not many in twenty years of marriage. Each lasted just a few months, and all over now.

As if in a time loop, the traffic light collapses again.

The pub steams and wartime camaraderie grips the clientele. Many are lorry drivers, trucks beached outside. Others are relatives stranded after visiting hour at the nearby hospital. There's a smell of dank coats and hair. Raucous singing begins in a corner and rapidly catches hold. The T.V. shows more scenes of the flooded city: circling helicopters and elderly people rescued into boats.

The old man's voice comes from a distance. His forehead beneath wispy nicotine stained hair is crinkled like cellophane. He gestures towards a young girl struggling through the crowded bar.

"Look at the arse on that!"

Taking out my mobile, I text my daughter again. The laborious search for tiny letters frustrates me, my fingers thick and clumsy on the keys. Lucy can't ignore a text. She complains my messages are abrupt, the modern equivalent of a caveman's 'Ug!' Our exchanges are an unequal ping-pong match. She says, "Get a grip, Dad. You're not ninety!"

But tonight there's no reply.

"There's one girl I remember," my companion slurs. "After the steel works laid me off I did odd jobs and that for a bit. I met her when I was round at her dad's cementing a step. A real cracker she was. Fifteen."

He needs no encouragement. I move the cribbage stick and think of Lucy; her quick silvery movements, her hair black glass. This morning her face appeared over my shoulder in the bathroom mirror, tongue protruding from the corner of her mouth as she applied eye liner.

"Do you have to wear that stuff to school, for God-sakes? Aren't you pop-eyed enough already?" I said.

"It's not for your benefit," she replied.

"And since when have you been taller than me?"

"Like my shoes, Dad? I'm going clubbing later."

She held out a slender foot for my admiration, turning the sandal from side to side.

"If you don't break an ankle first," I said.

The last stilettos in this house were miniature and plastic, wedged incongruously on the hooves of the grotesque multicoloured horses she used to collect and dress up. I felt sudden, unprecedented nostalgia for My Little Pony.

"Have you okay'd it with your mother? Going out on a school night and all that?"

"Yep."

"They say there's a storm coming."

"I'm not made of salt. I won't dissolve." She sounded just like Gemma.

Her eyes, stiffly fringed, regarded me in the mirror disdainfully. Then unexpectedly she hugged my back, smearing my shirt shoulder.

"No, but your mascara might run."

She had received a text and did not reply.

The old man is saying, "We had a great time in me caravan, I'm telling you." He stares at me. "What sort of father lets his daughter out after dark? Not in this city, not when there's all that wasteland. Anything could happen."

I wonder if it's normal these days for teenage girls to go clubbing in stilettos, eye makeup and not much else. I have no idea. What is clubbing actually? My opinion is never sought. I let my wife decide.

The ten o'clock news is sombre, the felled traffic light up-staged. The body of a thirteen year old boy has been found. He was swept away by a river in a nearby park. I know the spot, eat sandwiches there sometimes at lunchtime, recall a tame stream and toddlers paddling ankle deep. I don't recognise the devastated scene on T.V. — wilderness with trashed trees and a torrent roaring through. There's a school photo of a sturdy teenage lad.

"He just ran down to see the water. We didn't realise," his mother weeps.

The pub quietens briefly and then the singing resumes. I wonder when the storm hit our side of the city. In my imagination the front door swings open on an empty house.

"I didn't expect it to go so far," the old man says.

There are cigarette burns on his sleeves. I don't trust the light; his expression seems ordinary, pleasant.

"I helped the police search for her," he says. "They got some daft bugger to confess to it. He must have been gone in the head. Twenty years he got."

A door in my mind opens then bangs shut. There's a hollow rushing in my belly. I shove the cribbage board aside, stand up and push through the doughy crowd. A

147

man glares when I jog his elbow and beer slops over his glass, and then returns to gawping at the next news item. A young man has been trapped for hours with his foot wedged in a storm drain. He can't be freed and the flood is rising.

An onlooker says, "He was helping his neighbour rescue furniture. I know him — a nice guy."

I recognise the row of shops where I sometimes buy a newspaper. In front of the newsagent's, fire engines and an ambulance wait impotently. A paramedic supports the young man's chin above water. The camera pans across bobbing detritus: discarded nappies, toilet paper tangled round a stick and a rat's sodden corpse.

A highway of regret and longing stretches out in me. The news reader has hair like Lucy's. Like Gemma's too, before hers faded at the temples — it wouldn't occur to my distracted and ethereal wife to dye her hair. And for the first time, I admit she knew about those three women. Suffered and waited, trusting life to wash us to a more serene place. When we were young she used to weep over things — the plight of rain forests or the extinction of an orchid. She hasn't cried for years. I see what my carelessness has spoiled, like a musical instrument left in the rain. I would wade a thousand miles through flood water to get home.

The old man is beside me again. I smell beery breath and beneath that, something else. He sways and leans against me in a vile parody of intimacy.

"I think about it all the time," he says. His eyes glitter like fish scales.

"You're winding me up," I say. "You're not that thick. Why shouldn't I go straight to the police?"

"We're none of us going anywhere. Look outside. This is it, son. This is the end of everything."

News flash: doctors have decided to amputate the trapped boy's leg under water.

The old man says, "Nice guy, my arse. Stupid bastard more like."

I brush him away like a leathery insect and carve my way to the exit.

"You're crazy, pal," he shouts. "It's getting worse."

As I force the door open against the wind a triangle of light spills out over slanting rain and stinking, sludgy water. Beyond lies darkness and in the distance, the lament of sirens.

Salt disintegrates in rain. Dissolves and vanishes.

Staying Power

Wherever we go, we're too many. In small spaces the children seem to expand, filling every corner.

"We're not all like these people," the interpreter says to the doctor as we enter the room.

I chivvy the children before me, snatching at Ivan and Eva as they try to dart out again. Ivan puts his hand on the interpreter's knee. She stiffens and he springs away to rifle the wastepaper basket, tossing rubbish onto the carpet. The room feels packed and stuffy.

The doctor says, "Do you speak any English? Can you understand me?"

Nobody knows how hard I listen. Recently the strange sounds shifted and became words. I pretend not to understand because it's safer that way.

Eva coughs. The doctor catches her and pulls up her tee shirt to press a stethoscope to her chest.

"Have we got the right child here?"

Peering suspiciously at the screen he reads out the name of my cousin's child, Erik, who is pulling the paper roll from the couch to wrap around his brother.

"According to the computer this little girl, who looks about five, is a boy aged three. Are all these children yours?" he says.

The questions seem hostile because the interpreter doesn't look at me. I insist the name is correct and that all the children are mine. They are, in a way. My sisters' and cousins' kids belong to me too. Mine is the bed they migrate to at night, piling up around me in warm heaps.

When it gets too hot or they start fighting I sleep on the floor.

Erik presses buttons on the doctor's keyboard.

"Stop him doing that."

The interpreter's smile is stretched and mirthless. I gaze at her blankly. Back home women like this drive too close, splashing us, as they take their well dressed children to proper schools. Our kids are sent to places where they're allowed to fight and use the school yard as a toilet because there's no point trying to teach people who can't change.

Sometimes I'm afraid they're right. In the airport six months ago I looked at us, and doubted. The journey took less than a day. I couldn't believe it. Three hours from our village's dirt road to the airport; two countries separated by empty sky. There was no time to think because I had to stop the children running off to play in the toilets. Our baggage seemed wrong, tied up with rope. We looked different too, though I couldn't at first see why. At home they call us dark and dirty, but many people in the airport were darker. No two passengers looked the same, so various their clothes and appearances. My heart flew as I thought, we'll be all right now. Yet people were staring. I watched our men, eyes frosting with hostility, glare back, the little boys copying. Ivan aimed a kick at a suitcase. Soon there was space around us, everyone keeping their distance, fearful, as if we carried with us the smell of the place we left behind.

I want things different, my life to change. I'll never lie down for another drunk. I used to cry sometimes, even as I carefully folded the money, though I made sure Emil didn't see.

At the beginning he said, "What's all the fuss about? You've done it before, haven't you? It doesn't hurt."

Sometimes it did. But worse was that he imagined that life for me. And made it happen, denying where our money came from by getting drunk and shouting. I learned to retreat to a walled place in my mind, so that afterwards I remembered little. The men that wanted to kiss or talk as if I'd chosen them disgusted me. But nobody tried nasty stuff. Emil told them I carried a knife that I wasn't afraid to use.

Now I expect nothing from men. I love the children; my nieces and nephews flutter around me like moths. I've none of my own because the only time I fell pregnant, it went wrong. After three months I started to bleed, so Emil took me to hospital where I had an operation that nobody explained. I never got caught again. My sister said they probably did something to me under anaesthetic. They cut women like us to keep our numbers down.

No building contains us, we spill over. Other houses in the street hold three or four people, ours twenty or thirty. Nobody counts. Taking different children with us we move from house to house and back again. We go to the shops or doctors in groups of twelve or fifteen. The atmosphere changes as we enter. Darting around officials, swapping passports and identities, we carry confusion with us and know how to use it.

There are few hours when all the kids sleep, but some nights my bedroom, a riot of mattresses and leaping bodies, is quiet. I stand at the window with the city ringing in my ears and think, things are getting better. We've come a long way. We have tap water and a toilet that flushes, though I still have to nag the children that forget and squat in the yard or on the pavement. Usually I can herd most of them to school — a proper one with books, climbing frame and pictures on the walls. Dressed in clothes from the supermarket they look as good as the others.

The teacher says, "Can you understand me? Do you speak English?"

Not enough for her to grab me at home time to complain about Ivan. He claws and kicks the other boys as they scramble through the door. Eva and Stephania crouch in the playground, clothes awry and glowering, until I scoop them up to come home. They're so quick to anger and take offence that other children keep away. The mothers at the school gate avoid me.

Men that pass our house eye me up and down. I know that look. They believe I have no choice, but I've decided. Though Emil shouts, I'll not return to the dirt and mess of the years I left behind. Back home there's a door, so familiar I recall every crack on the paintwork. I used to hesitate outside aware I could turn back, yet always went in to the unknown man who waited. As if my body was a pile of sticks to be thrown, one by one, onto a fire that drew my life in.

Emil has started to inject. Thin and weak, eyes impenetrable dark circles, he's a slip-sliding disaster I do nothing to prevent. This time I see the cliff edge and he's not taking me with him. But when he's asleep I lie with my lips against his and feel the waste and loss of missing someone who never really existed. In my head I carry images full of light from another time, when he was my beautiful boy and none of this had happened.

Long ago he said, "I wish I had more arms so I could wrap them all around you, Rosa."

Most of the men have given up already. They lie in the splinters of all they've broken. Drunk on booze from the corner shop, they swagger and fight in the street. I try to stop the teenage girls picking up locals at the pub.

I say, "Wait, you don't have to. Things are better here."

I want a different life. My secret wish is to teach in a school where all children are treated the same. Ivan's classroom fills my thoughts, every paint pot, book and computer in its place. Like a shadow that comes and goes in faltering light, I see myself there.

We'll move on soon. I know from the neighbours' raised voices and shuttered faces. When they come to complain we scowl and shout, pretending not to understand. Rubbish is piled high on the pavement and in the back yard. Once the men decide, we'll move to another part of the city and start again. There's never discussion or plan, but overnight the group packs up and leaves. The children won't go to school one morning, and we'll not mention the teacher again.

One home time I arrive at school early. Peering through the window, I see Ivan sitting quietly on the floor by the teacher's chair as she reads the class a story. I hold my breath as I watch. He sucks his thumb and has the hem of her dress in his other hand, pressed against his cheek. Five minutes later he runs out of school with a sticker on his jumper. Although I understand nearly everything now, I can't read a word. A mother in religious dress, collecting her child, bends down and touches Ivan's badge. All but her eyes are covered, yet through the gap in her veil they crinkle in a smile.

"Good boy," she reads. "You must be. It says so here."

She walks part of the way home with me, her daughter hanging from my arm. Excitement moves inside me like a flurry of little hands because we understand each other. My first English conversation.

Next day at home time the teacher approaches me.

"I'm pleased with Ivan. He's starting to settle down."

This seems so unlikely, I think I've misunderstood.

She says, "Some parents come in and help me in the classroom. Would you like to do that? It would be good for Ivan to see we're on the same side."

I imagine myself with book on lap, calm and clever as the woman in front of me, reading a story to the class. From habit I keep my face neutral, but nod. Then I smile.

We come home to Emil slouched on the sofa, the other men scattered like spilled cards on the floor. I snatch the syringe out of the children's reach and for a second consider sticking the needle into Emil's chest. The room feels like that of a sick man who won't get better. Always when it's like this, we move on in search of the cure that eludes us.

I say, "I'm not coming this time. I'm staying here."

A hot tide races though my limbs then recedes, leaving me shivering. The men stir and look at Emil expectantly. They know they should have strong feelings about my treachery but can't, for the moment, locate them. He opens his eyes and stares at me. I sense fear wash quick and cold from his body to mine. He moves as if to stand, but the effort is too great. Saying nothing, his eyelids flutter and breath turns thick. And I tear him out. Like ripping paper: pinch the edges and pull. So easy I could have done it any time. Remembering all our collapsed hours, I don't know what to feel. Perhaps pity, because he can't live without me.

This morning I wake to an empty house. A new brightness bounces from every surface. Walking from room to room I take stock. Bottles and dirty plates scatter the floors, and a broken TV blocks the hall. All the adults have gone. They've taken Stephania and Irena, but Eva and little Erik are asleep in my bed in each other's arms. Downstairs a child is clattering about in the kitchen.

Ivan is shovelling cereal into his mouth from the box, his school book open on the table. Between mouthfuls he reads aloud in a faltering voice, pausing shyly for a moment when I come in. I stand behind him and look over his shoulder. As he runs his finger beneath the words they quicken with meaning. It doesn't look difficult.

I say, "Today I'm coming into school with you, to help the teacher."

He turns, takes my sleeve and holds it to his cheek. Thumb in mouth, he leans his head against me. I wish I had more arms so I could wrap them all around him.

JAM

Eve wasn't surprised. She had tried alternative routes and left home earlier, but her journey to work grew steadily longer. Accidents or bad weather made some days worse than others. She began to take food and books to pass time in jams.

And then the traffic stopped.

The first few hours were difficult. Eve fizzed with irritation, worrying about work and whether she'd locked her flat. Her manager, on the mobile, was resigned. Few staff had made it to the office that morning.

At first the traffic inched forwards but soon even this ceased and she turned off the engine. A helicopter circled overhead as she tuned to the traffic news. Across the country all vehicles were stationary. No one was going anywhere. As the day wore on drivers got out of their cars, proffered chewing gum and exchanged information. Children who walked past the jam on their way to school found it there when they came home. By evening entrepreneurs were weaving between vehicles to sell over-priced snacks and drinks to stranded commuters. As the sun melted behind the squat grey buildings that lined the ring-road, vehicles huddled, their occupants invisible behind misted glass. Darkness filled the car and drowned Eve in loneliness.

The nights that followed were better. She was prepared. She listened to the radio as traffic news became local, then national, news. After midnight the World Service talked endlessly about the jam, which had spread from country to

157

country. Nothing else was happening because no one could get to work. Journalists, politicians, criminals and celebrities were stranded and impotent. Wars stopped. International finance stopped. For long stretches of time the radio played only uplifting music or old dramas.

People wandered from car to car to pass time. Friendships and enmities formed and reformed. In the heightened emotional climate people fell in love, fought and betrayed one another. Rumours of events elsewhere in the jam circulated: rapes and robberies at gunpoint, anarchy and starvation — each more frightening than the last. Yet Eve's stretch of road was quiet, her main hardship boredom, which lay on her shoulders like a damp coat.

In the car adjacent to Eve's a man sat reading. He rarely looked up and never left his car. She studied his profile furtively. At last he closed the book and wound down his window.

"Have you got an A-Z?" he asked.

Eve invited him to sit in her passenger seat. Now she could see his right profile, which she liked as much as the left. When he turned to her and smiled the symmetry of the two halves pleased her even more. He introduced himself — 'Tim' — then ransacked her glove compartment for maps. Together they unpacked and studied every map they possessed. First, brooding over the city A-Z, they devised escape routes. When this palled they examined ordnance survey maps, pointing out holiday spots and homes of friends. As they talked the contours moved, pulsed and formed pictures. They pored over charts of countries they'd never seen, planning emigrations and new lives. Then, with maps plastered over the windows for privacy, they explored the cartography of each other's bodies.

Nights were different now. Sometimes the sky was black, depthless and impassive; other nights, stars wheeled across like reflections from a mirror ball. Neon light flickered on their faces as they talked. When the streetlights clicked off they were still making love. The World Service burbled in the background as they slipped through the cracks between night and morning.

The windscreen wipers whispered, "Life, life, life."

Eve gave birth beneath a blanket on the back seat. Assisted by another motorist, a nurse in former life, she stoically delivered three sturdy children, each a year apart. They fluttered at her breast like milk-crazed moths, until hardened enough to join the melee. It wasn't easy to raise a family in such cramped conditions. The car seethed like an overstocked carp pool. Eve and Tim learned to dodge flailing limbs and small hard heads. The children secreted a glue that coated the car interior and everything they touched, while crushed crisps formed a carpet ankle deep. Other parents were raising families in cars nearby. There were sleepovers and parties. You squashed eight children in a vehicle, pushed in three more small ones, stood back and watched it rock. Kids squabbled over sausages and hit one another, while dismembered dolls flew from windows and piled up outside. Eve and Tim began to look raddled.

Then between one breath and the next, the children collected rulers and pencils and leaping like porpoises, went to school. They didn't come back. Although she knew before they were born this would happen, Eve was lost for a while. They were good children. They sent texts from all over the world and flew overhead in aeroplanes from time to time.

One night she woke Tim. "Listen!"

Cool and clear, their youngest son was singing on the radio.

Meanwhile, bereft of workers the city decayed. Houses and shops near the ring road lost value; owners sold up, boarded the windows and moved away. Rats multiplied in the rubbish. Larger animals moved quietly in shadows. No one sat on car roofs through warm summer nights anymore. Vigilante groups formed to protect whatever property or children remained.

Usually Eve and Tim sat in her car together, but sometimes Tim preferred to stretch out alone in his. One day after he'd been gone some time, Eve glanced across and noticed his face altered. He'd moved the rear view mirror and seemed to be watching the woman in the car behind. His lips moved silently as if he was daydreaming. Eve went to the woman's car and peered in. She wasn't beautiful, but Eve imagined that beauty might move in someone who knew her. The woman glanced up and smiled. Eve smiled back uncertainly, returned to her car and waited.

Waiting, she held her breath. So hard, her breathing stopped. The hiss and whisper of air through her lungs that she'd heard without knowing every day of her life, hushed. Her heart stopped contracting as if gripped in a fist. Blood jammed up the little roads of her veins. She heard tiny creaks in muscles deprived of oxygen. The sound a heart makes when it isn't beating, but waiting. You can live like that, but not long. Dry because no saliva flowed, her mouth formed words that no one heard.

"Don't tell me."

Don't tell me. Because then. Because.

At last Tim got out of his car and back into Eve's, sighed and rested his face on her shoulder. Air warmed her nostrils, whistled and gurgled through her lungs. Stagnant blood began to flow and her heart to pump again. The first breath hurt like a razor down her chest — a violent, scarlet grief she would never express all the days of her life.

Day and night. Time binding and unbinding. Some hours expanded to fill a lifetime, others passed so quickly that meals and conversations flicked by like scenes from a train window. The space between days grew shorter all the time. Tim's hair turned grey, then white. His eyes shone with new glamour, but his edges had blurred. Sometimes Eve felt her name had slipped into a temporarily irrecoverable space. He searched their maps, unfolding and refolding the complex creases to find the right one, the first one, when their destination was clear, the journey's end assured. Their conversations fell like one-winged birds. Eve smoothed the lines from his forehead. She whispered their children's names, talked of all they had seen and pointed out aeroplanes passing overhead.

Still there was enough: oil rainbows on the road, windows laced with frost. They watched the moon's cool slide across the sky, the sun's bloody birth. More than enough, there was abundance. The best of all their days.

Eve woke one morning to new sounds: the throaty rasp of old engines, small explosions from rusty exhausts, traffic noise. People shouted and sounded their horns. Tim's line of traffic was moving and he with it. Confused, at first she thought her car was going backwards. Tim turned to her, his face through the glass anguished as his car picked up speed. She ran along beside, banged on the roof and tried to wrench open the door. But it all happened too fast. She was unfit, she couldn't breathe.

She was old.

She glimpsed things she hadn't seen before — a birthmark beneath his thinning hair, dents on the bumper — as the car pulled away.

Now the days rolled on faster and faster. Veins reared up on the backs of her hands. Her fingers twisted in stiff knots. Traffic to her right flowed freely. Inside her, a watchful eye of self remained unchanged.

So the day she woke to an empty road ahead she was ready. The key grated in the ignition but the engine fired at the third attempt. She wiggled the stiff gears and switched the lights on, off, on again. Her feet trembled on the pedals as the car began to move. The morning sky was a pale blue dome. Traffic lights changed up and down in an empty city. For the first time in her life Eve pushed the accelerator hard to the floor, feeling the wheels slip and engine whine.

She knew she would catch up with him at the lights. Or at the next glorious, dazzling traffic jam.